Sins of Another

JESSICA SKYE DAVIES

Dreamspinner Press

Published by
Dreamspinner Press
5032 Capital Circle SW
Ste 2, PMB# 279
Tallahassee, FL 32305-7886
USA
http://www.dreamspinnerpress.com/

Sins of Another
Copyright © 2013 by Jessica Skye Davies

Cover Art by Maria Fanning

ISBN: 978-1-62380-470-1
Digital ISBN: 978-1-62380-471-8

Printed in the United States of America
First Edition
April 2013

For Stanley, who showed me the meaning of unconditional.

And to those who have been there,
with thanks to all my friends who have encouraged and supported me
in so many ways.

FOREWORD

HELLO. My name is Padrig Kennedy. Padrig, not Patrick. I'm thirty-two now and have lived in East London all my life. I am *not* cockney, so just get that Eliza Doolittle shite out of your head. My friends call me Pad, not Paddy.

"What's in a name," right? Well, I find it pretty cool that so many experiences and feelings, the good and the bad, a whole life, can be summarized in a couple words. I've made the decision to share some of the experiences and feelings—good and bad—that have made my life what it is. I want people to know who *Padrig* was because I hope that, even when I'm not here anymore, maybe it could help.

Please stop for a moment just now, though. There's something important that I need to tell you before you go any further. Mine is not a cheerful story. I've been through a lot of very difficult things, some things that no one should ever experience, and some that no one should have to experience as frequently as I have in the last few years.

It's not always easy for me to talk about. It's taken me all this time to be able to look back, piece together the blank spots, and to face how it all felt at the moment. There have been times when I was thinking back on things that I actually felt a bit of a panic attack coming on, and I knew I had to step away from it for a while. I got past that, though, and came back to it because I knew this was something I needed to do.

But just as I feel it is important to warn you, I also want you to know that I am *not* an unhappy person. I know how fortunate I am. I would not want to waste that by being miserable about things I can't change. Life is too short for that sort of thing. I should know.

So, if you should choose to continue reading, I will describe my experiences thus far, shall I?

CHAPTER 1

FREDDIE and Archie have already been dropped off at their places, and I'm the last stop. After paying the driver my share of the fare, I hurry to get my bag from the back and jog up to the house. I fumble with the keys for a moment at the doorstep. Thinking that Nick is likely still in bed has me distracted; that's just where I want him to be because I'm planning to slip in beside him and sleep for the rest of the afternoon.

I wish he could have come with us, but his boss, Mr. "Nosey-Parker" Soames, insisted that he needed him to attend a legal conference for several days during the week that we were away. I did try not to resent Soames too much for it—Nick is their top paralegal and all—but he's got a bad habit of keeping tabs on Nick even during off-hours. Dodgy old bugger.

I sometimes have to remember that even though I'm not working, not everyone gets to pop off on holiday as they wish. Don't get the wrong idea—Nick is no sugar daddy and I would never treat him like one. It did actually make *sense* for me to quit my job selling upmarket menswear in Burlington Arcade. After I moved in with Nick, I had only a few monthly expenses that barely put a dent in Nick's salary. When your boyfriend says he wants to take care of you, you aren't likely to knock back the offer.

Nick felt that we'd have more fun without him along anyway, as he'd been cutting out drinking ever since that night he drove into our corner letterbox. I didn't see it that way, but I've never been the clingy sort. I can spend time with my mates without ringing Nick every hour, or he can join us and my mates don't have to feel like third and fourth wheels. Our relationship is healthy because we love and trust one another explicitly.

Just as I finally pluck out the front door key, I drop the whole set and shake my head at myself. I am a soppy sod. In my defense, I have just returned home from one of the most sexually charged places on earth, and I was without my partner the whole time. To be honest, though, it isn't even that I'm ragingly randy. I just want to be *beside* my lover again. I've gotten so used to snuggling with him at night that I ended up hugging a pillow to fall asleep the first few nights in Ibiza. Only pillows don't kiss you gently in the morning when you've got a massive hangover, or tell your mates to keep it down while you're recovering.

Anyway, I still had fun, and now I'm home. I set my bag inside by the door and head upstairs, making a detour to the bathroom first to wash my face. I know it sounds "metrosexual" as hell, but after a week's worth of sun, sand, salt water, and hotel soap, I'm really glad to be back to my own cleansers, toners, and scrubs.

Taking stock, I suppose I'm lucky I didn't come home looking like a cooked lobster, but I've definitely got a little more tan than my usual London pastiness. At least it makes my bog-standard-brown hair look a bit more interesting. I run a comb through, trying to tidy up the messy waves before giving it up. I'm due for a haircut, and it won't behave until I've had a shower anyway. That won't be happening till I've had my welcome-home snuggle.

Feeling "tingly clean and menthol fresh," I'm more ready than ever to get back to my own bed for a while. Crossing the hall, I push the bedroom door open just a bit. I'm trying to make sure I don't wake Nick, but I know that's a waste of effort. He could have slept through the Blitz without stirring. Peeking in, there's hardly any light coming through the heavy drapes, even though it's 10 o'clock on Sunday morning and actually quite bright outside.

The dull gray tinting makes the room look like a scene from a '40s film noir. I can see Nick sprawled over his side of the bed, facedown. He's dead to the world. His right arm is going to be tingly when he wakes up, hanging off the edge of the bed as it is.

Even a mess, his hair has always reminded me of smooth olive wood, and even in the dark the golden highlights of his chestnut coloring stand out. The sheet is wrapped around one long, toned leg, leaving the other exposed, along with his perfect, oh-so-touchable bum. He's gorgeous now in his midthirties, and he's got the sort of structure, a swimmer's physique, that makes it plain that he's going to be a dead-set hunk the older he gets. There are times when I see him, like now, and I just can't wait to grow old together.

Opening the door wide, I'm ready to shed my clothes before tucking Nick in properly and joining him. But then I see something that causes my world to change forever.

He's not alone.

Another man is in our bed. Sleeping on my side of the bed, the place where I've lain beside my lover for the last year.

The world stops. For a long moment, my mind can't process it. It's like seeing something that you are *sure* can't be real, even though it's right in front of you. I stand there in the doorway of our bedroom, breathing rapidly, my heart beating so loudly I'm surprised it hasn't woken Nick. My throat is tight, it's hard to swallow, and a burning in my chest is mirrored in my eyes as I try to keep tears from welling up. I can't stop staring at the sight before me, as if it'll go away if I just look harder.

The other man shifts and grunts softly, and I wonder if that sound means his arse is reminding him of the night before... hell, maybe it's been all week. I see him lift his head to look toward the doorway, but he doesn't make any move to get up. It's too dark to make out anything more about him.

And suddenly I feel sick, sicker than all the last week's hangovers put together. I've got a terrible, all-over cold, trembly feeling. My heart pounds and I feel like the blood has drained from my upper body. I just want to get away from this feeling, and the only thing I can think is that I need to be out of the house. Now.

I turn and run.

I run down the stairs and out the front door. I run to get away, down to the park, hoping I can find a solitary spot for a while. By the time I get to the park, I'm overwhelmed. I've managed to keep my tears at bay all the way down here. But now, as I sink down under a big, leafy birch, I just can't keep it in anymore. My mind is a clutter of "It can't be... he can't have... I must have been mistaken...." But I know better, I know what I saw. I saw the man I love more than anything in the world in bed with another man.

I can only take short gasping breaths around my sobs, but at that moment I don't even care if I can't breathe. It hurts so much, deep inside my chest, up through my tight throat; even the muscles of my face feel contorted in pain, and I've got a hammering headache.

I don't know how long I'm like that, lying against a tree, crying my guts out. I must look so pathetic. And it comes to me that maybe pathetic just suits me. That was what my first crush called me when I told him I fancied him, a "pathetic little faggot."

Someone comes walking by and stops when he sees me sitting there.

He stoops down to take a closer look at me. He's dressed very tidily and is well groomed, with dark hair and piercing gray eyes. Looks like a businessman on his way home, except that it's a Sunday morning.

"Hey, what's all this now?" he asks in a distinctly Brummie accent.

Stupid question, I think. It's clearly a pathetic faggot whose boyfriend, the one he loved more than anything, is probably still lying in bed with another man. Isn't that obvious to anyone?

"Please fuck off," I say to him as politely as possible. I realize that considering how weak and scratchy my voice is, he probably didn't catch it anyway.

"Here, lad," he says softly, offering me a tissue. "Come on, now. It can't be as bad as all that."

I take the tissue, but just hold it in my hand. I guess all this crying has made my nose a bit runny, and that only adds to the overall pathetic-ness of the picture I present.

"It is, that bad," I rasp. "So please let me alone."

"Well, if I do that and then hear it on the evening news that a gorgeous young man hopped off a bridge this afternoon, I'd feel rather like shite. Likely worse than you're feeling now."

Why the hell won't he shut up and go away? I've had my heart ripped from my body; do I really need some wanker bothering me now as well? No, I fucking do not.

"Come on, lad," he tries again. "Sitting here crying won't solve it anyway, now will it? Let me get you a cuppa, shall I? I only live about a couple hundred yards from the other end of the park."

"Yeah, alright," I say. Hopefully it'll get him to go home and leave me alone. Then I can find some other place to bury my shattered heart while he's off making tea.

"Good." He stands up but doesn't go away. He just stands there like he's waiting for me. Bugger.

With a sigh, I finally wipe the tears and snot from my face, wishing I had that toner that's back in the bathroom cabinet right now. But I'm not going back there. Not for a while. Maybe in a few days. I'll have to at least tell Nick I'm leaving him.

Oh hell. Am I going to start crying again every time his name pops into my head?

"Come here," the guy says as he offers his hand to pull me up. He wraps me in a hug and rubs his hands over my shoulders, softly shushing me. "Come on, love, come and talk with me. It'll get better, I promise."

I rather doubt that, but despite still wishing he'd just leave me alone in my misery, it kinda does feel better to have someone hold on to me. He starts walking us along, keeping me close and steering us toward his place. I briefly wonder why I'm letting a total stranger take me back to his place for tea. Isn't this just the sort of thing that gets people into bad situations? I'm so miserable and exhausted right now that I don't care.

CHAPTER
2

THE guy leads me across the park, keeping his arm around my shoulders. He's decent enough to not talk much along the way. Maybe my headache shows on my face. We cross a couple of streets to a neighborhood of nice houses, fully detached and a bit more upmarket than our neighborhood. He seems well off and like a genuinely nice guy. He leads me into his lounge and returns shortly with two cups of tea.

Sitting beside me, he says, "So, what's upsetting you, lad?"

I glance at him briefly before returning my gaze to my knees. It's like he really wants to know, like he really cares. Part of me wonders why anybody would care about some loser sitting in a park, bawling his eyes out.

My weary thoughts wander away from the lounge and the man being so generous to me. The ache in my chest hasn't faded, and by now I've worked it out that my heart is well and truly broken. I start tearing up again as I get a mental image of my sweet boyfriend lying there in our bed, dead to the world. Then I see the form in bed beside him and I want to be ill.

I wonder if Nick is awake yet, if he knows I'm back from holiday or that I ran out of the house. I left my bag in the hallway; what will he think when he finds it there and doesn't find me? Will he be looking for me? What would he say to me if he found me? "Sorry 'bout that" wouldn't cut it. What would, however, I don't know.

I just want there to be an explanation. I want for him to come running after me and tell me that I was mistaken, that it was only his brother who unexpectedly came to stay. But Nick is an only child.

"It helps to talk," the guy says, and he lays a gentle hand on my arm. I'd forgotten he was even there. "We can start out easy. What's your name, lad?"

I take a sip of tea, hoping it will ease my sore throat. It's brewed strong and bracing. "Padrig," I answer quietly.

"Padrig, then. Does anyone know where you are? Your girlfriend, perhaps?"

"Don't guess so. And I had a b-boyfriend… until this morning."

"You prefer blokes?"

"Yes," I reply tightly. I guess I can still sometimes be touchy about admitting to strangers I'm gay.

"He doesn't know where you are or that you're upset?" he asks me concernedly. "He's probably worried about you."

"No. He doesn't know. He didn't even wake up when I came home." Once again I feel that crushing sensation in my chest. But then I find myself turning angry. "And if he's worried then it's his own bloody problem!"

How could he have done this to me? What could have driven him to sleep with someone else just because I was gone for a week? I was in bloody *Ibiza*, but I managed to remain faithful, because I love him and don't want anyone else.

What if I never want anyone else? What if I'm still in love with him when I'm like fifty, even knowing that he cheated on me so easily?

"You two had a row, then?" the man asks me.

"Not yet," I mumble. There won't be any rows. I'm not going to shout at him and make it ugly when I leave. I'm just going to say good-…. Fuck me; I can't even finish the word in my head without choking up.

"What happened?"

"He cheated," I whisper, before downing some more tea. "Found him in bed with someone else when I got home from holiday this morning."

"Bugger, lad. That's terrible." He wraps an arm around my shoulders in sympathy.

"That sums it up," I say around an unexpected yawn. I'm starting to feel really tired. No surprise, I *was* planning on crawling in bed and sleeping for a while when I got home. Unfortunately, there wasn't any room for me in bed.

I'm thinking I should probably thank the guy for the tea and for being so nice to me, and then ring up Freddie. I'm going to need a place to crash, and Fred owes me about a hundred favors. Wait till he hears I'm calling them in all at once.

"Listen. Thanks a lot, mate…," I say to the guy, and I finish off my cup of tea. I can't just keep referring to him like that. Not after he's been so decent. "Um… I'm sorry I'm being really rude, but I didn't get your name."

"I'm Bennett," he says, offering his hand. I take it, but don't give much of a handshake. I'm so exhausted even clasping hands seems like a major expense of energy.

"Bennett. Thanks for everything. I mean the tea, and talking to me. It's really made me feel better."

"You're welcome, Padrig," Bennett says. "Just for the record, I think your boyfriend doesn't deserve you. He's a fool and an arse to want someone else, even for a moment. You're very attractive, and you seem awfully decent."

I still feel like I've been cast headlong into a deep, dark, cold hole in the ground, but that is a nice thing for him to say.

I stand up and he does likewise. "Are you going?" he asks, disappointed.

"I think. I've got to ring my mate and tell him what's happened. He'll have the pleasure of putting up with a heartbroken friend for a few days, at least until I'm feeling brave enough to face Nick again."

"You look tired, Padrig," Bennett says. He reaches out and holds my arm at the elbow when I sway slightly on my feet.

"Yeah. I am a bit," I nod. Fuck. That makes me dizzy. I'm feeling really strange, like I've come down with a fever. I feel way too hot, but I'm shivering and feel weak. What the fuck…?

"Why don't you stay here a bit longer? You can ring your friend when you're feeling better," Bennett says. "Just sit down and relax. Let me get you another cuppa."

I sit back down, but I don't relax. I get a dizzy, sickening, whirling sensation, like a looming, dark vortex is spinning around me. I feel the room tilt and I'm sure I'm going to slide off the sofa any moment. I feel completely disconnected from everything, even myself. That's when I black out.

CHAPTER 3

THE next thing I'm aware of is feeling sick. I'm talking horrendous. I feel nauseated and I'm afraid to as much as flinch for fear that I'll throw up everything down to my toenails. I must be hungover. Have we left Ibiza yet? I don't dare open my eyes with the raging headache I've got.

"Freddie," I rasp, "Haven't we got to get to the airport?" I try to ignore the bile rising in my throat as I talk. I really want to be home again, but I'm not looking forward to flying while feeling like this. I might have to take one of Archie's sedatives if I'm not feeling better by the time we get to the airport.

I shift my leg very carefully, trying to move without being ill. I manage to keep my stomach from doing backflips, but then I notice a particular soreness farther up between my legs. There's no mistaking that feeling. Someone fucked me last night. More than once, I'd bet. But Nick's not here with us. Does this mean I…?

I rummage through my foggy memory, trying to figure out how I could have gotten so drunk I'd bring someone back to the hotel. And then I remember that we're not in Ibiza; we came home. Was it yesterday? Did Nick and I get that drunk to celebrate me being back?

I feel so confused; I don't remember hardly anything except getting out of the taxi and hurrying up to the door. What did I do then? Went in, right? Okay. Was Nick up, having brekkie, waiting for me? My mind wanders to how nice that must have been, having Nick's arms around me as soon as I walked in, and some lovely Heinz beans and toast on the cooker. Did he tell me how much he's missed me while kissing my neck in that way that makes me shiver all over?

No, that's not what I did. I went upstairs and washed my face. Right, because Nick would still be having a lie-in. So I'd have just gone and snuggled with him in bed. Okay, I remember that now, seeing him lying in the dark, the sheets all messed up around him. I went in and covered him up properly before joining him, right?

Oh God. My memory, for a brief but intense flash, is clear. Nick was with someone else. I felt like shite before, but now I feel heartbroken as well as sick. I don't want to think about it anymore. I wonder where I am though. Most likely at Freddie's, but I don't remember coming here. All I remember is crying in the park and some guy who felt sorry for me and offered tea. Everything after that is a total blank.

I finally decide to risk escalating my headache for the sake of opening my eyes. I have no clue where I am. This definitely isn't Freddie's flat, or Archie's. This room is Spartan. There's the bed I'm on and a little nightstand a few feet away. Rather defeats the purpose as it's just out of reach from the bed. There's also a blue, plain-looking armchair in the corner opposite and one window, covered by a roller shade. The floor is bare. That's it. No drapes, no pictures on the beige walls, nothing decorative.

For a while I feel too sick and sad and weak to bother putting two and two together. Nick cheated, and I'm in a strange place. I remember fuck all, but I must've had a hell of a time last night. Eventually I get the impression I must have gotten drunk and gone home with someone out of revenge. What other conclusion can I come to, waking up face down with an aching arse in a strange room, all after learning my boyfriend cheated on me?

The whole thing is too much for me at the moment. My heart is breaking all over again, and this time it's my own fault. I never meant to sleep with someone else. I'm angry and disappointed with myself for running off. I should have tried to talk to Nick first. Instead I acted like an immature prat. Our relationship was stronger than that. I might have walked away for a while to cool down, but we could have worked things out.

Swallowing down all the sickness and pain, I push myself to sit up. I'm going to get dressed, apologize to whoever's bed this is, and go directly home. Nick and I need to have a long, mature discussion.

Step one, however, is immediately thwarted as I can't find my clothes. There are no clothes lying around at all, and no dresser or closet doors. I guess whoever I was with thought he'd wash them for me or something. Well, obviously he's seen all of me already. I'll just have to ignore my nakedness and go seek him out.

Actually getting out of bed makes me feel even worse. I can't ever remember a hangover that made me feel this bad, and I wonder if I've come down with flu. My muscles ache as I stagger nakedly toward the door. It hurts to grasp the knob. I tug at it but nothing happens. I turn the knob but it doesn't move. I fumble around for a moment, feeling for a lock of some sort, but there's none on this side.

Why the hell is the door locked?

"Hello?" I knock at the door as I call out, even though it makes my head feel like it's bursting and hurts my knuckles and makes me feel like I'm going to vomit. I wait for a moment, leaning against the door for support. Then I try calling out a little louder and knocking harder.

I'm draped against the door like a ragged old dressing gown on a hook, recovering from my exertions, when I hear someone coming up the stairs. The footsteps stop outside the bedroom door, and there's the whispered scraping of a key inserted into a lock. I move back just as the door is opened and a big, strong guy with dark hair and beady eyes steps in. I went home with this guy? I must have been truly ratted; he's not even remotely my type.

He just stands there, arms folded over his chest, his back to the door.

I really feel naked now and find myself stepping back toward the bed with a nervous swallow.

"Um… look, mate, last night. I don't remember much of it, to be honest, but… I'm really sorry about this and all, but it was a mistake. I really shouldn't have, I was just upset about my boyfriend. Guess I thought this would be revenge, but… it was a stupid thing to do and I don't blame you for being narked with me. I just… I need to get going."

The guy shakes his head slowly and steps toward me. "No, you don't need to be going anywhere for a while. You're going to be staying right here until North decides you're ready for the market."

I look at the guy like he's grown another head. Who is North, and why doesn't he go to the market for himself?

"Listen, really, I am sorry about last night. But I need to go home. I can't be playing this like it's a game of tit-for-tat."

The guy grins. "Oh no, it's definitely not a game." He's scary. I wish he wouldn't look at me like I'm breakfast.

"Yeah, so, if you could just get me my clothes, please."

He keeps grinning though, and a moment later another bloke comes in. He's not as big, and his hair is a shade lighter. His eyes are a piercing gray. I recognize him from yesterday, the one who found me in the park and took me home for a cup of tea. Something is really wrong here, but I can't think clearly through feeling so sick.

"Sleep well, Padrig?" the smaller guy says. I don't remember his name. "Alex, hold him," he instructs the bigger man.

I don't react for a moment as the big guy comes toward me and tightly grasps my naked arms. I can't seem to process anything clearly, and I'm starting to feel agitated and upset.

"I want to leave." I realize as the words leave my mouth how weak I sound.

"No," the smaller man says in a soothing tone. "You aren't ready for that just yet. It'll take some time."

I shake my head, trying to clear my thoughts. "What are you talking about?"

He doesn't respond, and Alex holds on to me tighter. He must be bruising my arms as he walks me backward until my legs hit the bedside. He pushes me down and panic finally hits me. I need to fight back. I thrash, trying to get free of Alex's grip. But it's useless; he is much stronger than me. I try kicking instead, hoping to hit something sensitive that will make him let go of me for a moment.

Alex shifts and uses his body weight to keep my legs pinned. He then takes my wrists, stretching my arms out. The other guy steps to the headboard and produces a length of rope tied to the bedpost. He ties my wrist and goes round to do the same with the other one. Alex is still straddling my legs, and he's got a malicious look in his eyes.

I'm shaking so hard I can only stammer as I beg them to stop. I pull frantically at the ropes, but it does nothing. This all seems unreal to me, but the pain and sickness I feel tells me that it's not just a bad dream. These men are trying to keep me here, tied and naked. My breath starts coming in gasps, and all I can think is that I would never be in this situation if I'd just stayed calm and talked to Nick instead of running away.

Oh God, Nick! Please, find me and I'll stand aside while you sleep with whoever you want. I don't care, just save me from this!

I must have said that out loud because Alex snickers at me. He leans in and kisses me hard, forcing his tongue into my mouth. I try to resist, but as uncoordinated as I am it doesn't help. Then I feel a sharp stab in my arm, and I scream against Alex's mouth.

"Don't moan so bloody much," the other guy says. "It's just a little prick of diamorphine, you'll get used to it soon." I hear a little metallic clink, like a needle being dropped into a glass bottle.

I start to sob as the injection site throbs. I've always been scared of needles, and these men mean to use them on me frequently. I try to struggle again, but the ropes just feel tighter and my arms feel heavy. I feel dizzy and warm all over, even though I'm naked. I don't like this at all. I've never done drugs in my life, and I don't know what they're injecting me with.

"Why are you doing this?" I try to ask. They just laugh at me.

"Don't worry now, lad," says the one who injected me. "When this stuff wears off you'll get some more. And when that's not enough we'll get you some other goodies as well." He looks at Alex, who's finally moved off me. "You took care of the text messages?"

"Sorted, Ben'et. Sent one to the boyfriend saying he knows everything and isn't coming back, and one to the friends telling them he's lying low because of the boyfriend."

"Brilliant. Keep those going, you know what to do."

"Don't worry. Time I'm done, his mates will think he's the biggest arse in the world. This'll go off without a hitch."

"We certainly got just what we were after. Might even have to send the barrister a nice fruit hamper," the guy called Bennett says smugly as they walk out of the room and close the door behind them.

I can only lie there, feeling hot, heavy, and high. I had my mobile with me, my wallet and passport as well. They sent messages to Nick and my mates… they won't be looking for me. I feel so sleepy and confused, but I'm so scared. I keep trying to pull at the ropes and call for help until my throat hurts and all I can do is cough weakly.

Nothing happens. No one comes for me.

I'm left with the feeling that no one ever will.

CHAPTER
4

A LOT of things are unclear for me during this time. I don't have very good recollection of the majority of what happened. I have impressions that are mostly vague and general. There are only a few things that stand out as clear to me, and rarely for good reasons. I have no real concept of time; I don't know how long I've been here. I can only tell day from night based on whether there's any light coming in from the edges of the roller-blind over the window. I don't leave the bedroom, and they don't open the window shade.

I try to keep my thoughts together, to keep track of what's been happening to me or what seems to be going on. It's difficult though. Very little happens to me, really, but I can't keep it straight in my mind, and that frightens me more than anything else has yet. I mentioned being highly needle-phobic, but my worst fear, the thing I've had the most nightmares about, is having my wits robbed from me.

Often, my head aches whenever I wake up or make it out of the heavy, gray fog that surrounds me most of the time. It feels like my brain has been replaced by cotton wool. I just can't get two thoughts together. I'm tired from my head on down. It's too much effort to try to think.

Bennett and Alex only come back in to inject me. The first few times my arms are still spread, kept tied to the bedposts. My arms have gone numb, and I can't feel it when Bennett presses the needle into my flesh. I still struggle, and it robs me of what little energy I had. There's a momentary rush, and then I'm disorientated, shaking, and scared.

I want to try to think of a way to get out of here, but I can't. Instead I just lay there, my arms sore from numbness, my head aching and heavy, tears dampening my face. My brain cells fire off a last message before the drug takes me into oblivion for a while—if this goes on much longer, I probably won't care anymore.

Over the first few days, I think they injected me a couple of times daily. It all becomes very routine, which I think contributes to my confusion over how long I'm there. What's really strange about it is that every time they come in, Bennett is very kind and professional, like a trusted doctor. He acts almost sympathetic toward me, as he did from the moment he met me in the park. Underneath it all, though, is a sinister sort of efficiency.

The other guy, Alex... I've had nothing but roughness and sneering from him. I'm so weak that I can hardly resist when they come with the needles now, but he still grasps my arms tightly and pins me down. There are bruises on my arms, at my biceps and wrists, as well as at the injection sites. Every time Alex is in the room, I feel even more anxious. It's like he's just waiting for Bennett to leave him alone with me. He wants to hurt me.

They stop keeping me tied to the bed after the first few days or so. The first time they leave me untied, I struggle to get up off the bed as soon as they lock the door behind them. I can't stand on my own, and collapse to the floor. I drag myself over to the window. I don't care how many floors up it is, or if I'm too weak to climb down. If I can just get *outside*, I have a chance.

There's no way to get the window open. It's a fixed pane of glass. I think of trying to break it. I pound at it with my fists, but either I'm too weak or it's made of Plexiglas. Likely both. I curl up against the wall under the window, wondering if anyone would see me if I stood there in the window, naked as I am. Would they call the cops about indecent exposure? Could that save me, or just make everything worse? It doesn't matter; I'm not strong enough to stand there for long enough to attract the attention of some nosey neighbor.

Bennett and Alex find me lying there on the cold, polished wooden floor under the window. Alex picks me up and tosses me back onto the bed. Bennett sits down on the bed beside me and strokes my dull, grimy hair. I realize how filthy I feel; I haven't bathed in days. What a thing to worry about at a time like this.

"Oh, Padrig. There's no way out," Bennett says. "Not yet, at least. You aren't ready for outings. We'll take you when you are. I know this is all difficult now, but before long you'll be partying even more than you did in Ibiza. A lot more."

Bennett then turns to Alex. "I think we can get him started on the meth. You can test ride him for the next few days, then we'll see if we can get some clients set up by next week."

I KNOW this is horrible to say, but I preferred the meth. When Bennett put it in me, anally, it felt a lot better than the heroin. No needles, and I didn't get that disorientated feeling. I felt brilliant. I didn't care that Alex held me down and fucked me; in fact I wanted it. I felt like the best little sex toy anyone ever had. Bennett sat by and watched, cackling loudly when I cried out Nick's name as Alex jerked me off.

AFTERWARD, they leave me there alone again. I feel hollow and so cold. I curl up on the bed and pull the blanket around me as I begin to sob. I want Nick. I want his arms around me again. I want his warm scent on the pillow. I want to hear his soft voice tell me that I am safe and everything will be all right again. I want him to tell me that he loves me and will never leave. I lay there and cry until I crash. And it's exactly the same every time they put that stuff in me.

Over the next few days Bennett only comes in to inject me; he doesn't often give me meth. Every time Bennett leaves, Alex comes in. He always tells me the same thing—he's not interested in me, it's North he wants to fuck, he's only using me because I'm available and will soon be valuable to him. He tells me about sending text messages to my mates, pretending to be me and convincing them that I'm fine, that I want to be left alone to "lick my wounds." Alex makes sure to tell me that none of them seem to be concerned about me at all.

I've noticed that I no longer feel unwashed. I don't remember being bathed. I also begin to wonder about food. I don't really think about being hungry, but surely I must be getting some kind of nutrition. One day when I come out of it, I realize I'm in jeans. They're rather loose on me, and I'm not sure what the point is of me wearing them anyway. That same day, Alex comes in, not to fuck me, but to bring me soup and bread. I feel almost normal, getting to eat food and wear clothes. If only I didn't feel drugged all the time.

From then on, Alex brings me soup a couple times a day. It's not very good, really bland vegetable soup with just a bit of meat in, and the bread is a bit stale, but it's good enough for me and I eat it eagerly. Alex also bathes me every couple days after the drugs put me to sleep. He says I'm not trusted to shower on my own, in case I try to drown myself. Alex also tells me that they plan on keeping the meth for special occasions, like when they have a client lined up for me.

I don't realize what he means until the first time Alex doses me with meth just before Bennett brings another man into the room and leaves him alone with me. He doesn't say anything to me, just turns me over and fucks me. He knocks on the door when he's done and hands Bennett money.

I don't think I'll ever really be able to comprehend the progression from one day being a perfectly happy, healthy man in a fulfilling relationship with a good social life... and the next being a drugged-up whore. It's not like I made bad choices in my life. Did I?

Time goes on. Weeks, months? I don't know, have no way of knowing. Every day is the same for me. I'm drugged. Many nights some guy or guys are brought up to fuck me. I am never told anything about it. I never know how many it will be, or when. They don't talk to me, and I don't talk to them. Most of the time, I'm already facedown on the bed and I never even see them. They just grab my hips and go to it until they finish, then leave. They're usually drunk; I can smell the alcohol.

Some of them touch me, but they're not interested in getting me off. It makes me moan though, and some of them like that. If there's one who's brought in late, when the high has started to wear off, I sometimes come while they're fucking me. It's difficult to feel even an orgasm through the drugs.

I usually don't get much recovery time. When one is done with me, the next one is brought in. They don't waste much lube on me either. Sometimes it hurts the next morning, if I'm coherent enough to notice the pain. Sometimes I wake up with a sheet stuck to my back or belly from dried come.

At first, I tried to tell myself to pretend it was Nick making love with me. I gave that up pretty quickly though. It only resulted in me sobbing while some stranger shoved his cock inside me. So then I tried not to think of Nick at all. There's not really any chance I'll ever see him again. I gave up hope a long time ago of him saving me from this. I try not to torture myself with the knowledge that we could have just talked about it.

I don't bother trying to look out the window or wonder if summer is ending yet. Sometimes I wonder, despite what Alex said about the text messages, how my friends could really think I was just feeling sorry for myself. Wouldn't they want to know where I am so they could at least come round and visit? I've given up thinking about that as well though. Most likely they've written me off as a hopeless case and moved on. Pathetic little faggot, once again.

But just when I'm starting to get used to the human sex toy routine, fate has another curve coming for me.

CHAPTER 5

THE light is pale at the edges of the roller-blind. Bennett and Alex never bring anyone here to fuck me this early. Morning usually means food or an injection. Today, they bring something different as well—new clothes. I would be excited about that, if I had the ability to get excited about anything without the meth. Even then I'm not really excited, just chemically stimulated. Certainly not happy.

These things are really shiny, and tight as all hell. I don't wear them right away, though. It's not until that evening that Alex dresses me up. I had thought that perhaps they had a client who wanted a nicely wrapped sex toy, but then Bennett did something that totally shocked me: he had Alex take me out of the house.

If I were in my right mind, I would have figured out some way of getting away, at all costs. I'm hardly in my mind at all though; the afternoon heroin hit hasn't worn off yet. I just sit in the backseat, my head lolled against the headrest. I stare up into the dark night, blinking against the harsh streetlights as Alex drives through the city. I don't recognize anything; it's all just a blur going by. Other cars, buildings and shops, people. None of it has a meaning to me; it's all surreal. This is the first time I've been outdoors since that morning in the park, and I don't even know what's happening to me.

Alex stops in front of a very flashy, very loud nightclub. He unlocks the car door from the outside (the locks inside have been removed), and he "helps" me out. He keeps a tight hold on my arm, like a sadistic chaperone, as we walk by the bouncer who nods to Alex.

He doesn't need to hold on to me like I'm going to run away. It would be ridiculous if I tried. I'd probably stumble after three steps and just lie there on the pavement not realizing anything was wrong. At this point, I remember nearly nothing of what was "normal." The only thing I do recall with any clarity is Nick, no matter how I try to forget.

Inside the club, Alex pulls me over to a table and sits me down. He gives me a pill and I take it. They haven't given me the meth anally in a long time. Alex smokes a cigarette and watches the room for a few minutes. Then he pulls me up and onto the dance floor. This is the most fucked-up date I've ever been on. There are people all around us, mostly male, grinding and bumping and wriggling. We're not here to have fun, though. I soon learn that this is business.

A middle-aged man with spiky platinum-blond hair comes up to Alex and gestures from himself to me. The noise level in the club is way too high for talking, so Alex responds in gestures. First he holds up his splayed hand, then indicates "one." Then he points to his mouth and indicates "two." Without warning, he slaps my vinyl-clad arse and indicates "five." It takes me a few moments to realize Alex is giving the other man a price list. The guy points to his mouth and counts out a stack of ten-pound notes into Alex's waiting palm.

Having checked the money, Alex grabs my arm and ushers me across the club. I'm disorientated by the pill he gave me anyway; the strobe lights and thick smoke only make it worse. Alex pulls aside a heavy curtain from a doorway to reveal a plush little room, and he pushes me in ahead of him. He leans against the wall as the spiky-haired blond pushes me down to my knees. "Spike" settles himself in a comfortable leather chair and leans back, unzipping his trousers and taking out his hard cock.

He reaches out for me, grabbing my shoulder and pulling me in between his legs. "'Ave a taste, darlin'," he says. His voice is like muddy rubber tires rolling over even muddier gravel. He puts his hand on the back of my head, and it's only then that I realize my hair is extremely short now. I can feel his hot, sweaty palm against my scalp, and I wonder what I look like. My hair must be buzzed off almost completely.

Spike gets impatient with me and the next thing I know, he's shoving his cock between my lips. It's the first time I've had a penis in my mouth since I was sixteen. I didn't like it then and I've refused to do it since. I guess that was pretty disappointing for most of the guys I dated, all except Nick. He understood that I wasn't comfortable going down, and he never pushed me about it.

That's why it's strange that when Spike pushes in, I don't hesitate. I go to it like it's an oasis in the desert. And it seems that I've lost my gag reflex as well. It doesn't take long before he shouts out and comes copiously down my throat.

It goes on for the rest of the night like that. I don't leave the room. Alex shows one client out and comes back in with the next. I don't know how many there are, but it is more than they bring to the bedroom. I'm exhausted and sore by the time Alex escorts me back home. The drug he gave me has worn off, and I'm left coming down as I compliantly wash my face under Alex's supervision before he locks me in the bedroom again. There's nothing for me to do but get in bed and sleep.

Most days they continue bringing clients to the bedroom. Alex takes me to the nightclub only occasionally. It might be weekly, I'm not sure. I think they're dosing me frequently now, but Bennett hasn't used needles on me in quite some time. Things are getting less and less clear to me all the time. I mostly give blowjobs at the nightclub; it's rare that they want full-on sex there. It's just the opposite up in the bedroom. I don't think anyone ever paid for just a hand job from me.

There are times when I space out and don't know what's going on around me at all. I don't know that I'm being fucked in a loud, smoky nightclub. I don't know that I'm anywhere at all. I haven't passed out, but I just go off into nothingness. Sometimes Nick is there in that nothingness, reaching his hand out to me. I'm always too fucked up to take it.

ONE time when Alex takes me to the club, Bennett comes along. He doesn't stick around to watch though; as soon as we're in the club, he goes up a spiral stair to the second level. I'm left with Alex giving me a pill and "dancing" with me, which I've realized is meant to be an advert, until the first bidder approaches. I'm taken over to the curtained room to give a blowjob.

I feel really strange. More than usual. I don't know if Alex has given me something different or if it's just a stronger hit. When the guy comes in my mouth I choke on it; it makes me feel sick. I don't say anything though. I doubt it would do me any good. I feel like I'm spiraling way out of control. My heart is racing; I wouldn't be surprised to see it pop out of my chest. I'm sweating like I've run a marathon. My head feels completely disconnected from my body. I'm scared. I want to tell Alex I need a break but he's already bringing in the next client.

Bennett steps into the room just then and stops him. I think that maybe he's going to let me have a rest; maybe he knows there's something wrong this time. I've worked it out that he knows about medicine, and that's why he was the one that always injected me. Instead of a rest, though, Bennett has another client who he says is to go ahead of the one with Alex. The first guy protests, but one look from the new client silences him and he leaves quickly. I just lay there watching, tightly gripping one of the pillows on the futon.

This man looks wealthy, nothing at all like the drunk businessmen I'm used to. I know it's been some time since I worked at the shop in Burlington Arcade, but I remember what an upmarket suit looks like. This guy is groomed to surgical precision, and his eyes have a clarity and focus that are unnerving. A long, deep, jagged scar from the corner of his mouth to his right ear makes you not want to question what happened to "the other guy."

"I want this man to have as much time as he likes with our little *commodity*," Bennett says to Alex. "He is very influential, and I'd have you treat him as one of us." I've never heard Bennett speak so obsequiously.

The man in the posh suit walks over to me as I'm struggling to pull myself upright. He looks at me for a long moment, giving me a thorough once-over. His eyes, despite their sharpness, hold nothing even remotely readable. He takes me by the arm and pulls me up to stand. I feel dizzy and almost fall down, but he holds me up and starts to walk me out into the club.

"Hold it, mate," Alex says, trying to stop him.

Bennett looks like he's about to rebuke Alex, obviously wanting to impress the other man by letting him have special privileges with me. Before Bennett can say anything, though, the scarred man steps close to Alex. He doesn't speak very loudly, but I'm sure Alex hears every word perfectly even over the din of the club.

"What? You think I'm going to fuck in a filthy hole in the wall? If I wanted that, I'd come to your whorehouse." The man's voice is harsh, but his accent is somehow warm.

He then leads me across the club and ushers me up the spiral stairs. I'm sure I'm going to slip and fall down them any moment, but he keeps a strong hold on me. Bennett and Alex follow us. On the second level of the club, the man takes me over to another room and opens the door. He gestures for me to go in ahead of him. Left without him holding me upright, I stagger inside the dim room, grasping around as I hope to find something to hang on to. I feel like the whole room is tilting around me.

Alex tries to step into the room as well, but the man stops him.

"The twink isn't supposed to leave my sight," Alex protests.

"This is the second time tonight you insult me," the man responds evenly. "I am no exhibitionist. Who do you think the whore is here, anyway? I can find plenty of other London boys to fuck, you know."

"Alex!" Bennett growls. "Our friend is worthy of our trust. My apologies, Mr. Zinov—"

The man cuts him off with a curt wave. "I will let you know when I am done with him," he says calmly. He leaves Bennett and Alex outside the room to wait in the hallway.

I'm stood against the wall, hoping this Mr. Zinov-something is planning to bend me over a table or chair. I don't think I can support my own weight much longer. In fact, I'm not sure I'm going to be conscious much longer. Or ever again. It's difficult to concentrate on what's going on, but I have the feeling that my life may depend on it. Something is different about all this.

This guy is a lot scarier than Alex and Bennett. I don't know what he's planning on doing to me. I just hope he's like most of the guys who don't expect me to participate or respond to them. He reaches out and puts a hand on my shoulder. I wait to feel him push me to my knees, but he doesn't.

I begin to shake all over. I'm drenched in sweat. My heartbeat feels erratic, and my ears are ringing. I think I'm going to pass out soon.

"You are not well," the man says quietly. "Can you walk?"

I just look at him. His question doesn't make sense to me. The only word that leaves my lips is a shaky "please."

"Come here with me," he says. He wraps an arm around my waist and guides me across the room, not the way we came in. He opens a door and cool air surrounds me. We are outside. I don't know what's happening, and I'm too sick and scared to ask. He helps me down an iron stairway and takes me over to a sleek black sedan that's parked there in the alleyway. He opens a back door and helps me inside.

"He is very sick," he tells a man sitting in the driver's seat. "We must hurry. Make certain that he is safe and then come quickly after me." He shrugs off his suit jacket, takes something folded like bedsheets from beside me, and closes the car door.

The driver gets out and locks the car doors. For a second I wonder what twist fate is giving me now, can I try to get away? But then I realize it doesn't matter anymore. I'm dying. I don't know how I know, but I do. I'm sure that I only have maybe an hour left in me and that I won't be aware of most it. I'm losing consciousness as I lean my head against the cool, black window.

True to his word, Mr. Zinov-whatever doesn't take long. I vaguely register something heavy being dropped into the boot, twice, before it's slammed shut. The driver gets behind the wheel, and Mr. Z gets into the back seat with me, instructing the driver to "go immediately to St. Becket." His shirt is spattered with dark stains, and he takes it off, changing it for another that he takes from a compartment in the back of the driver's seat. "If you want it done right, sometimes you have to do it yourself," he says to me.

My last thought is of Nick. I miss him so much. I just wish I could see him one more time, to say good-bye.

CHAPTER
6

I DON'T know what's happening to me, but I'm certain I'm dying. I had hoped I wouldn't have to be conscious of it at the end, or that at least it wouldn't hurt. I've always been afraid of death, down deep in a place I've tried not to go.

I don't know where I am. I don't know if there's anyone around, but I feel alone. I wish I had a friend here, but I haven't had a friend in a long time. I try to call out for help, but all that comes out is a squeaky croak. Who would help me anyway? Maybe Bennett or Alex would if they knew they were losing a source of income.

I don't know where I am or what's happening to me. I'm not really in touch with my senses. I seem to go in and out of being barely conscious. The only thing I know for sure is that everything hurts. I feel like I've been tortured or beaten almost to death. I feel so sick, like someone's tied up all my insides into a thousand knots, and then beat them against a brick wall like an old dustcloth.

I shake as well. All-out, violent tremors wrack my hurting, exhausted body. I have no energy left at all. Sometimes I'm so cold I shiver; other times I sweat so much I feel like I'm lying in a pond. When I try to swallow, my mouth is dry and my throat is raw. It feels like I've been screaming myself hoarse. Maybe I have been and just didn't know it.

Sometimes I think there's someone there, around me. I can't seem to open my eyes all the way or see well; it's all bleary. Everything I sense is vague. My hearing is like a radio trying to pick up a signal from too far away. I can tell someone is saying something, but I don't know what or who it is, or if they're talking to me. Truth is, I don't feel that I can be sure there's really anyone there. I don't trust my mind too much at the moment.

THE hurting has almost all gone. I don't feel like I'm sick all over. I don't feel like I'm falling down a crevasse, plunging headlong into hell. It's like waking up on a Sunday morning after a long night. I don't feel like bouncing out of bed; I'm still rather sick, but I feel okay. Okay is the best I've felt in a long time.

I lie still for a long while, enjoying the feeling. I'm still pretty tired. I don't think I'll be awake long. Slowly, I'm becoming aware of my surroundings. There's a soft, steady beeping coming from somewhere behind me. The bed is hard with stiff sheets. The pillow under my head feels like vinyl covered in cotton. It's chilly in here. This isn't the bedroom I've been in for so long.

I open my eyes just a little. White walls, faux-wood fixtures, pale-blue printed linens, hard tile floors, and devices attached to the wall beside me. Not to mention this hideous "gown" I'm wearing. I'm in hospital. I don't remember getting here, and I'm surprised I'm alive.

What does this mean? I try to remember as much as I can. How long was I in that room? Don't go there, my mind tells me, slamming that door. Okay, there was the nightclub. And a client, really posh. I was really sick. He put me in his car. I don't know anything else. Did that guy bring me here? Is he expecting to take me with him when I'm released? Or are Bennett and Alex waiting for me to be released?

No. I'm away from them, all of them. I'll kill myself before I let them take me again. This is a hospital; I'm safe for now. I can get the police, go someplace safe. They won't get me again, that's all there is to it.

Then I think of something else. What if I could find Nick? Maybe we could talk, be together again. Just thinking of him makes me smile and feel good.

But the feeling doesn't last long. How could I ever tell him what happened to me? How could he ever accept me, knowing what I was like all that time?

I don't feel better at all; I feel worse. I try to curl up on my side but feel something tugging at my hand. There's an IV taped into my hand. I shudder deeply and can't control it when tears slip down my face. I hate needles so much. Just when I thought I was away from them, that I was finally safe, the fucking things are still haunting me. I want to rip it out, but I know it'll hurt. Instead I'm left with that "squicked" feeling. It doesn't really hurt, but I know it's there, *in* my skin. I turn my head away, trying as hard as I can to ignore it.

"Hello there." A woman's voice. A nurse, I guess. I glance up to see a tall, pretty woman with long, dark hair. She's wearing white and is surrounded by light from the doorway. If it weren't for the IV in my hand, I might think I was dead after all.

"You look like an angel."

She smiles and comes over to take my hand. "Sometimes my husband calls me that, I'm really just a doctor. Dr. Sharma-Penston, you can call me Dr. Asha if you like. I was really glad when the nurse told me you seemed to be awake."

"I thought I was dying." I realize how disappointed I sound.

"No, you're going to be alright, Padrig. I understand if you're still tired, so if you want to get some rest, that's fine. I'll be around later as well. Or if you'd like to talk with me now, we can."

"I am tired. How do you know my name?" No one but Bennett has said my name in so long; it's strange to hear it again.

"Do you remember how you got here?" she asks.

I shake my head.

"The gentleman who brought you had your wallet and passport, as well as a mobile phone."

"What happened?"

The doctor sits in a chair beside the bed. "You had a pretty bad overdose. It was touch and go for a while. Do you remember taking any drugs?"

I nod and try to swallow down a lump in my throat.

"Can you tell me anything about it?"

I don't want to remember any of it. "They gave me... um, heroin at first, I think. And meth. There might have been other things, but I don't know for sure. I never really knew what they were doing to me."

"You didn't take anything on your own?"

"No! I didn't want to be there, I wanted to go home! They kept me locked up, and drugged up, constantly." It's the strongest reaction I've had to anything since I ran out of the house that morning.

"I'm sorry, Padrig. I truly am. I promise you're safe here. You've done well. What was in your system when you arrived has mostly metabolized over the few days you've been here and you're really on the road to full recovery. I have every confidence in you. I'd like to bring along one of my colleagues when I come by later. His name is Jarrod; he's a psych doc. A little unconventional, but one of the best guys I work with. He can talk to you about a lot of things that I'm not as good at. Would that be okay with you?"

"Okay." I don't really want to talk to anyone at the moment. I just want to burrow into my sterile hospital pillow and forget everything for a while.

"Okay, good. Is there anything I get you before I go? Another blanket, perhaps?"

"Yeah, please."

"Sure. Anything else?"

It feels so strange asking for things, even just a blanket, after so long. And she's a doctor, not room service. She seems really nice though, and I really want a second pillow because only one of these vinyl cushions is unbearable. "Could I get another pillow as well, maybe?"

"Definitely," Dr. Asha says. She seems to not mind at all. I have no reason to mistrust her, none at all. But for some reason, I just can't trust her completely. I feel sorry for that. And it worries me. Will I be able to trust people again, if I'm really through this?

I'm a lot more comfortable after Dr. Asha brings the pillow and blanket. I don't want to lie here and just think, which I'm sure I will with time on my hands. I'm tired anyway; maybe I can just sleep for a while and not have to think.

I'VE been awake for a little while when Dr. Asha comes back a few hours later. There's a guy with her, who I guess is the other doctor she mentioned. He's kind of weird looking, though, not at all what I'd expect from a doctor. He's got streaky, shaggy hair, a moustache and goatee, a general laid-back sort of style.

"Heya, Padrig!" He greets me in a Northern Irish brogue, as if we're old mates. He takes off his hat that looks like a relic of 1945 and hangs it on an unused IV hanger, then reaches his hand out to me.

I take it, despite being mildly baffled by his general disposition.

"I'm Jarrod. Some people insist on calling me Dr. Ambrose, but I find that to be far too pretentious. Anyway, I'm really glad to meet you. Looking forward to getting to know you."

"Do you think you'd like to talk with us?" Dr. Asha asks me. "I'd like to go over some information about your diagnoses, if you're up to it."

"Alright," I say, but my guard is up. Something about the way she says "diagnoses" bothers me. I was under the impression that all I had to do was rest up. She said earlier that there weren't drugs in my system anymore.

"One thing is that we want to make sure you've got support in case you have any longer-term withdrawal issues. You've gotten through the majority of the symptoms from the substances identified in your system; that's behind you. It is possible that you might experience 'cravings' for some of the substances, but with good support you can get past that too."

"No. I'll never want anything like that in me again, not for as long as I live. I hated it, every moment. Do I have to have this in me now?" I nod toward my left hand with the IV in it. I've avoided looking at it so far.

"Not necessarily. Now that you're awake and lucid, we can take you off the IV and start getting you onto more standard nutrition routes."

"Padrig," Jarrod says, "I couldn't help noticing, you seem agitated about the IV needle."

"I am." I can't help squirming just responding to him about it. "I'm afraid of needles. I was before, but I hate them even more now."

"Okay. We'll keep that in mind with any medication options we might look into with you, okay?"

"Thanks."

"Padrig, I also need to talk to you about some test results," Dr. Asha says. "Because of the circumstances of your admission, we ran a pretty comprehensive battery of tests to better understand your health status and how we could best treat you. I want you to know that other than some nutritional deficiencies, which the IV will have pretty much reversed, your tests came back with generally clear results. However, the test for HIV antibodies came back positive."

CHAPTER
7

FOR a few moments I don't understand what she's said. My tests came back generally clear… but I tested positive on the HIV test. Positive….

Positive. It's supposed to be a good thing, right? Positive— optimistic, certain, encouraging. Of course I know better. I'm a gay man; I grew up in the '80s. I know what HIV *positive* means, and it *doesn't* mean a good thing.

"What?" I ask in a strained whisper. Maybe I heard her wrong. My heart is pounding, and it feels like my whole body is begging for someone to "say it isn't so." My throat feels tight as I'm literally trying to swallow this information. I'm trembling.

"You tested positive for the presence of HIV in your bloodstream, Padrig," Dr. Asha says.

"Take your time, Padrig," Jarrod says softly, compassion in his voice.

I lay my head back and turn my face away from the two doctors. I can't say what's going through my mind, everything and nothing.

"I'm so sorry," Dr. Asha says quietly. She sounds like she really is sorry. For a moment I don't pay any attention, but then I feel angry.

"What do you mean you're sorry?" I say hoarsely. "Why the fuck are you telling me this?"

"Because you need to know, Padrig," Jarrod says.

"You let me think I'm getting clean, that I was finally free of what they did to me. I started to think I had some kind of chance!

Why… why didn't you just let me die?" Neither of them answers me right away.

"I don't know all of your circumstances, of course," Jarrod says calmly, "but I think you've probably had a lot of choices taken away from you. Deciding to die is a pretty big one. Not really our call to make, as doctors. The fact is, Padrig, you're living now, and you do have a chance. You have a lot of chances. You aren't at an end here, but a beginning."

I turn back to glare at him.

"Padrig, Jarrod's right," Dr. Asha says. "You are alive, and you're a fighter. You have a lot of living to do. Your choices are yours from now on, and we want to help you by giving you as much information as you need to make the choices that you feel are right for you."

I turn my glare to her. "What about getting this out of me?" I ask, raising my left hand.

"Absolutely," Dr. Asha says. Jarrod offers to go fetch a phlebotomist. "I can do it," she says, clipping the IV tube, putting on a pair of latex gloves, and taking my hand in hers. "Relax your hand as much as you can, okay, Padrig?"

Jarrod immediately comes to the other side of the bed and offers me his hand to grasp. "I hate 'em too, know how it feels. Concentrate on me and breathe."

It seems childish to me, but I take his hand and hold it tightly. I feel the pinch as Dr. Asha removes the needle, and Jarrod grips my hand a little tighter.

"Alright, the needle is gone. I'll put a little antibiotic cream with a pain reducer on that and it should be a lot better soon, okay?"

I feel relief wash through me to have that thing out of me. Then I start crying, and it's everything—relief to be away from Bennett and Alex, and to not be drugged, and to have that IV out of me; gratitude to Dr. Asha and Jarrod, and guilt for how I've acted with them so far; and whatever it is I'm feeling about being told I'm HIV positive. I'm confused and scared and worried. I don't know how they can say this isn't an ending for me.

I haven't let go of Jarrod's hand. "Take as long as you need, Padrig," he says softly. "We're here for as long as you need us."

"Thank you." My voice is so raspy. "I'm sorry, I just… there's so much…."

"It's okay, Padrig, you haven't done anything wrong," Jarrod says.

"But I've been so hostile with you both, and you're just trying to help me. I guess I really need the help because I… I don't know what to do."

"We *are* here to help, we'll do anything we can to work with you, Padrig," Dr. Asha says.

"That's a normal reaction, Padrig," Jarrod assured me. "A lot of people react similarly, and most of them have said to me that it takes a little time to process things and adjust, but once they do it gets easier to deal with. You don't have to deal with anything on your own, we're here and there are a lot of other resources as well."

"We can talk about the medical side of your diagnosis, if you have any questions," Dr. Asha says. "I understand that you may feel pretty overwhelmed right now."

"Yeah… I kind of am."

"I have a lot of information I can leave for you, that way you can look at it in your own time and process it. We can talk about any questions you have for me whenever you're ready."

"Okay. Um…." There's one thing on my mind more than anything else at the moment. "I don't want to be in hospital forever, or even another day, but… I'm not sure where I'll go. When I'm released."

"I thought maybe you and I could talk about that," Jarrod says. "I'm hoping we can talk more about your previous situation later on, but I also wanted to let you know about Willowmead, the place I work. It's a really unique place, kind of a community center, kind of a care facility. You could have your own private flat, totally individual care, all the freedom you want. It's a nice place, quiet and comfortable, secure, really healthy environment."

That last bit is appealing to me, but I don't want to say I'll go and be packed off to this place first thing in the morning either. He might say it's nice, only for it to turn out to be a dreary prison for the dying. "Do I have to decide now?"

"You do not, definitely not," Jarrod says. "In fact, we can go visit sometime in the next few days if you want to. You should be able to see Willowmead for yourself before you make any decisions."

"How long will I be in here?"

"I'd like for you to stay for a few more days," Dr. Asha says. "We want to make sure your systems are stable and we can get you back to taking regular nutrition, and that you have a good place to be released to. I want to tell you, Padrig, I really believe in you. You have a special spark. Is there anything you want to ask me about, or talk to me about just now?"

"I can't think of anything at the moment."

"Okay. I'll leave some information for you here." She sets a stack of papers and leaflets on the nightstand. "I'm going to let you have some time to talk with Jarrod if you like. I'll be in to see you tomorrow and we can talk more then if you want to, all right?"

Nodding, I remember something as she reaches to clasp my hand once more. "Did you say my wallet and mobile were brought in?"

"Yes, when you were admitted, as well as your passport. Would you like them brought to you?"

"Yes, please. And thank you."

"You're welcome, Padrig. Try to get some rest, okay? I'll see you tomorrow."

Dr. Asha leaves, and after a few moments Jarrod says to me, "I know this may sound like a stupid question to be asking, but can you tell me what you're thinking just now?"

We'd be here all night if I were to answer that fully. "A thousand things."

"You've got a lot to process, I can tell. I'm hoping we can work together on that through time."

"How much do you know about what happened to me?"

"Not much. I've been told that you were brought here several days ago after an overdose. According to the admission papers, the person who brought you in informed the staff that you'd been in involuntary sex work for a while. Other than that I only know your name. And really, just knowing those things doesn't tell me anything about who Padrig Kennedy is. Only you can talk to me about who you are and what you've experienced, and what you're experiencing now, and what your hopes and goals for the future are."

"I was so relieved to be away from them. I guess I didn't think at the moment I'd have to deal with everything anyway, but still, I thought... I'm outta there, I've got a chance, can get my life back."

"It takes time, you don't have to work through it all at once," Jarrod says. "And your life *is* your own. We can talk about anything you want to pursue. Hell, if you want to go to the moon, I can give NASA over in the States a ring and ask 'em about what your first steps should be."

Jarrod succeeds in getting a laugh, albeit a small one, out of me. It's probably the first time I've laughed since Ibiza. The laugh slips into a yawn.

"I know when I'm boring my audience," Jarrod says with a self-deprecating smirk. "If you'd like me to go and let you have your rest, just say."

"I am tired. Feel like I've done nothing but sleep in so long."

"Your body is recovering from a lot. But you'll get your strength up again, just take it easy for now."

There are so many thoughts in my mind, it's hard to tell if I will be able to sleep. Hopefully my mind will be merciful.

Jarrod fetches his vintage fedora from the IV hanger and offers me his hand. "Asha's right about you, you're a fighter. And I'm pleased to know you. I was thinking I could come by tomorrow after breakfast and maybe we could talk some more, if you're feeling up to it. Doesn't have to be about anything particular, just whatever."

"Okay."

"If you need anything, go ahead and ring the nurses. And more than anything, just remember, Padrig—you're not alone in this. I'll see you tomorrow."

After Jarrod leaves it takes me a while to get to sleep, even though I feel tired. A nurse bringing in my wallet and stuff draws me out of almost being asleep. They stay untouched with the papers from Dr. Asha; I'm just not ready to look at them.

There's a window set in an alcove to my right. The vertical blinds are open, but it's dark out. There's a light reflecting from what I guess is the walkway below, and it illuminates the slender top branches of a tree. The leaves are still small, and I realize it's spring.

In the dark, in that uncomfortable hospital bed, those sticky sensors on my chest, a hundred questions occupy my mind. How long will I live? What am I supposed to do with what's left of my life?

What's funny is that I don't think I had the answers to those questions before everything happened, but I always assumed I had "all my life" ahead of me. I'd figure it out. Even when I was kept locked up, one thing that kept me hanging on when I had no other reason was the thought that if I got out of there I'd have the rest of my life to take back.

Do I have only myself to blame? Wasn't it ultimately my fault? I reacted so poorly to finding Nick in bed with another man. And I never should have gone along with Bennett and taken his tea. Do those mistakes merit my paying with my life?

It's too much for me to deal with. I wonder if Jarrod really can help me get through this. I want to get through it; I want so badly to have some kind of life again. I don't want to be miserable for the rest of my life—however long that will be.

But just now, pulling the blankets up over my head and hiding from the monsters of the world sounds like a really good idea.

CHAPTER 8

THERE are some mornings when you can't coax your brain to come up with a thought for love or money. You exist in a quasi-slumber for half the morning. Then there are those mornings when your brain is ready to go before you open your eyes, and it has a very definite agenda for you.

"Maybe there's some mistake," is my first thought this morning. There's such a thing as a false positive. The odds are really stacked against that, though. Who knows how clean those needles were? As for condoms, I was too messed up to know if they were used even half the time.

A nurse wheeling a computer cart with lots of drawers in it pulls me out of my thoughts, and for that I'm grateful.

"Good morning, Mr. Kennedy. Dr. Sharma says you're off the IV now, is that right?"

"Yeah, thank fuck. Oh, sorry."

She smiles like a sister who promises not to tell mum. "She has you down for taking some vitamin supplements instead, so I guess you're not going to be getting a good English breakfast just yet." She brings a dose cup with about five pills in and hands it to me, before turning to fetch a cup of water.

"Are these safe?" It's hard to believe I'm nervous about taking *vitamins*.

"They are. The bigger yellow one is a B-complex, which has several of the B vitamins in. The white one is a vitamin C, the round one is vitamin D, the orange is a vitamin A, and the green one is vitamin K."

"They don't have anything else in them, just the vitamins?"

"That's right, there's no other medicinal stuff in them."

"Okay. Thanks. I don't mean to sound paranoid." Taking the cup of water, I swallow down the pills. It's hard not to brace myself for feeling an uncomfortable high set in.

"Don't worry about it," she says. "You're scheduled to have another dose of these same ones in the evening. I think Dr. Sharma will be round to see you sometime after breakfast. Do you need anything?"

"I don't think so. Thanks though."

"No problem, Mr. Kennedy. Just ring if you need anything, okay?"

"Yeah."

She stops outside the door and types something into the computer for a moment before moving on. She seemed so at ease with me I wonder if she knows I've been diagnosed with HIV. I know she couldn't get it just being around me, but when I was growing up HIV was talked about like leprosy.

She mentioned breakfast, which doesn't really make me hungry just now, but does make me wonder when I'll be back to eating properly. I was fed by Bennett and Alex, if not very well. I was thin but fit before; I know I'm not fit at all now, and it seems to me like I'm way too skinny.

I still feel tired, but I don't feel as groggy as I did yesterday. It's strange to feel like I'm not completely in a drug-induced fog all the time. It does make me think I might be able to live on my own terms again. My worry is that it will take time for me to get back on my feet, but time is no longer my ally.

This bed must really need to be oiled; it makes a horrid whinge whenever I push the button to raise the head so I can sit up and wash my face from the basin. I'm thinking it would be nice to have a shave and shower soon too. There's a telly up on the wall in front of me. Maybe it can distract me for a while. It's too early to have so much on my mind. After a few minutes of scanning the stations, I realize that there was one thing I never missed while locked up in that room—midmorning programming.

Putting the clicker on the bedside table, I'm greeted with that stack of leaflets and my wallet, passport, and mobile. It's hard to say which I'm more nervous about picking up. The leaflets, at least, are sure to contain impersonal facts. Maybe I can meet this head-on. There are those stories you hear about people living into their 70s with HIV, and even dying of plain old age. Maybe if I learn all I can, and work every day to be the healthiest I can be, maybe my life doesn't have to be cut short. Maybe I'll even have time to fall in love again.

I wish I hadn't thought that. Suddenly I miss Nick so much it hurts. It hurts to miss him and it hurts to remember that last time I saw him. Maybe I haven't felt the full impact yet, but I swear seeing him in bed with another man hurt more than being told I've got HIV.

Hoping once again to distract myself from my thoughts, I pick up a few of the leaflets. Most of the information is basic stuff that almost any gay man my age should already know. The information about treatments is probably the scariest stuff. I've heard about how the meds can make you pretty sick, but I can't imagine having to deal with the side effects every single day. I'm pretty averse to taking anything ever again at this point, but I know I'm going to have to find some way to get over that. Not treating this is clearly not an option.

A soft knock at the door, Dr. Asha, makes me glad to put the leaflets aside.

"Good morning, Padrig. How are you doing today?"

A shrug says it all. "I'm okay I guess."

"You seem more alert today, that's good. And I see you've had a look at the information I left. We can talk about any questions you have, if you like."

There is one question that's been bothering me more than the others. It takes me a moment, I'm not sure I want to hear the answer, but I know I need to. "Do you know how far along I am, how long I have?"

"I can give you some clear answers about that, but there are a lot of factors involved. When you were brought in and we ran tests, your

CD4 count was running borderline low and your viral load was elevated."

"I… don't really understand what those things mean." It's a sad feeling, and I'm a bit afraid that I'm going to start tearing up. All these things that I never knew about my body—I guess most people know they have an immune system and red blood cells and stuff, but who ever knows they've got these "CD4" things streaming around in them and that it's very bad if they get too low?

"It's okay, Padrig. If I get ahead, please don't be afraid to tell me," Dr. Asha says. She takes a seat beside my bed. "CD4 is a protein on immune system cells. What HIV does, very basically, is to break into immune cells by attacking that protein and then making changes in the cell to use it to attack other cells. When this chain effect spreads, it shows up in blood work as having fewer cells than normal with the CD4 protein. So when we test your CD4 levels, we get a sample of how many cells still have that CD4 protein. Normally it should be between 500-1000. Lower than that is when we suspect a problem with the immune system. Your level was right around 375, which is pretty close to the level when it's recommended to look into treatment. If the level goes below 200, that's the mark that is often used to define AIDS.

"Now, your count being at 375 doesn't exactly say anything about 'how far along' you are. Counts can and very often do change a lot over the course of time. I've had patients slip under 200 and then rebound. There is a lot of uncertainty with HIV, and I know that can be scary, but I also find it hopeful. This stuff is changeable, something we can work together on.

"It's also really common to ask how long you have to live, but it's almost impossible for me to give an answer to that. I know that doesn't do you much good, and I'm sorry. The thing is, I could tell you years or decades as a best case scenario, or a few months at worst, and be dead wrong either way. It depends so much on how your body responds and how you take care of yourself. But there again, nothing is exactly certain. I've seen patients do everything 'right' who just didn't respond to treatments, and I have patients who do things *nobody* should be doing with their health and they are managing rather well. Just personally, I believe that your mentality has as much to do with it as your body. That's why I work with and highly recommend Jarrod. He's outstanding."

"Do you really think I have a chance? If I take good care of myself, could I... rebuild a life?"

"That I can answer. Definitely, Padrig. There are some things that will be different in your life, yes, but there is no reason you couldn't live normally and do almost anything you want to do."

Her confidence is genuine; it's rare to hear such conviction from anyone.

"We'll work together to get your strength back up, I promise. Do you think you'd like to discuss treatment options? There are a lot of things to work on that we can integrate as well like dietary and nutritional stuff."

"Would it be better for me to talk about it right now?"

"We don't have to; I can stop back later today, or even tomorrow. It's entirely up to you. Right now the focus is on getting you recuperated. It's not immediately necessary for you to start any treatment, and we won't do anything until you've got all the information you need to make an informed decision. Right now I've just got you down for vitamin supplements so that you can get what your body needs without the IV. I'll have them send you up some light soup for lunch and we'll see how that goes for you. Make sure you keep taking small sips on the water too."

"Okay. Thanks."

"Alright, Padrig. Jarrod will be around to say hello sometime today, I do believe. You take some rest until then, okay? We'll talk some more whenever you're ready."

She is so patient with me. It's such a change from doctors who try to tell you everything within fifteen minutes and then rush away before you're able to even think of any questions. Like when I was fourteen and in hospital with pneumonia.

I hadn't realized until she mentioned soup that I am really hungry. Bennett and Alex didn't quite starve me, but they didn't waste much food on me either. I probably haven't had anything to eat since the last time I was in that room. I've got nothing to do until lunch, and though I could probably just close my eyes and sleep, I don't really want to do that too much. Talking with Dr. Asha, even though she couldn't give me definite answers on everything, has made me feel a little more like I've at least got some… well, maybe not power, but I've at least got some say in my life again.

On that little wave of strength, I decide to pick up my mobile and wallet, two everyday items that contain so much of our personal identity. Most people take them for granted (until they're halfway to work and realize they've left them on the dresser), but I haven't laid eyes on these in months. How they were recovered I don't know.

Surprisingly, my wallet still has my identification, bank card, credit card, and a variety of membership cards. There's even a fiver in there. The only thing that I can tell is missing is my photo of Nick and me.

Then there's my phone. Turning it on, I'm surprised to find it's almost fully charged. Was it true what Alex so enjoyed telling me? That he sent messages to my friends telling them that I was fine, and that they were never worried or wanted to see me? What else did they do with my phone?

There are voice messages, mostly from Nick and mostly from around the time everything happened. A few are from Fred and a couple from Archie. A couple more recent ones are from Nick, including one at Christmas. They've all already been listened to, because they aren't showing on the list in bold print. I'm not ready to hear them.

There are text messages too, a lot more of them. Thinking it'd be easier to read than to listen to my mates' voices, I open Freddie's thread. And that's when I learn the extent of what Bennett and Alex were doing when they sent those messages. They were effectively separating me from any support I might have if I ever got away from them. The messages they sent under my name are mean, bitter, and angry, and they make it seem as if I blame Fred and Archie for Nick cheating.

One of the last text messages from Fred says very clearly what he thinks of me:

"I never knew you were really such an arsehole. Fuck off and stay fucked off."

They took everything from me. They took my freedom, they took my pride, they took my mates, they took my health. They took my life and all that it once was. I just wish I knew why they did it. Why me?

CHAPTER 9

THE soup I'm given for lunch is typical hospital food, bland and slightly disgusting. I know this is a key step in getting me out of here though. I still don't really know what "out of here" entails. Clearly I've no longer got friends I can stay with until I'm back on my feet. I guess that place Jarrod mentioned is an option, but I'm feeling so down after having read those text messages that thinking positively is a challenge right now.

Before I can get too bogged down by that train of thought, there's a tap at the door and Jarrod steps in. He's got the same vintage hat he wore yesterday in his hand and tosses it at the empty IV stand with a flourish, saying, "Hey, Padrig. How's it going today?"

"A bit better. Well, a bit better, a bit worse."

"Totally understandable. So, is it like, better in some things, worse in others?"

"Pretty much."

Jarrod nods. "Mind if I sit?"

I shake my head.

"So what have I missed since yesterday? What things are better than they were then?"

"I guess I feel a little better about trying to get myself back together. I'm not going to be dead by week's end, so I kind of have to do something about my life. Can't just lie here, and definitely don't want to."

"Good. I'm glad to hear that," Jarrod says with a confident smile.

"I'm also allowed to eat. Which is a good step, but this isn't exactly the Savoy Grill either."

"Well I could probably nip down to The Strand and bring you a nice hanger steak, but you might not thank me for it later. And Sha-Sha would probably bludgeon me."

"Sha-Sha?"

Jarrod shrugs and grins. "Asha Sharma, Sha-Sha. I'm a complete eejit. Some damn fool years ago gave me a paper saying I'm a doctor, no idea what they were thinking of!"

This guy is definitely interesting, I'll give him that.

"Now that I've got you grinning, do you want to mention what's not as good since yesterday? I promise I'll try to quit faffin' about."

"Honestly it's just been since I had a look at my phone earlier. I didn't listen to the voice messages, 'cause I didn't think I could deal with that just yet, but I read some of the texts. It was a bit of a mistake."

"Why is that?"

"Because the two bastards who kept me locked up.... This is a long story."

"That's alright, I've got all day."

"They sent text messages to my mates, telling them what happened with Nick, and that I just wanted to be on my own. Then whenever my mates started asking where I was staying and if I was okay, they started sending ones that blamed my mates for helping get me out of the country so Nick could have his... fling. Made me sound like a complete arse."

"That's certainly some shit," he says, shaking his head.

"Yeah."

"I wonder would you mind running it back a bit though? I'm only just coming in on the second act, so I've missed the cast of characters and all. Who's Nick?"

"He *was* my boyfriend." I'm glad Jarrod made me laugh a moment ago, because I'm certainly turning morose by now. "I was on holiday in Ibiza with my best mates, Freddie and Archie, for a week. When I got back home, I found Nick in bed with some other guy. And my reaction is what led to me being drugged and prostituted for months."

"How so?"

"I ran out of the house and ended up sitting in the park crying. That's where this guy, Bennett, found me."

"What happened?"

"He acted like he felt sorry for me and wanted to cheer me up. Offered me tea and I went back to his with him. I drank a cup, told him why I was upset, and next thing I knew I was...." Fuck. This is hard to talk about. I'm glad Jarrod closed the door behind him when he came in.

"I can tell it's difficult," he says quietly. "Take your time, Pad."

"I was...." I hate how your throat closes up when you get upset, how you can only get out a few words at a time and how words feel like stones in your throat. "Locked up and drugged up. Stupidest fucking thing I've ever done."

"There's a really big difference between 'stupid' and 'vulnerable'," Jarrod says.

"Yeah, well, who the hell knew there are kidnappers who go around drugging inconsolable guys over twenty-five?"

"Most people don't know much at all about human trafficking. It happens more than anyone cares to know, not just girls or people in developing countries either. I don't claim to have seen a lot of cases, but I hear of it more than most people do. Some places in the world, nearly half of trafficking victims are male."

"This seemed... *individual*, though. Like they were only interested in me. I think I remember, or maybe hallucinated, I don't know... them saying things like they got just what they were after. I don't know why though. I know I'm safe here, but I'm kind of worried about them trying to find me after I'm released. But for some reason, I don't think they're still alive."

I don't say anything for a while. I have a vague memory of the man who took me out of the club that night having blood on his shirt when he returned to the car. I decide I'd really rather not go down that road now.

"What's on your mind, Pad?" Jarrod asks after a bit.

"Just that I don't want to think about it right now. Maybe later. If they're dead, I can't be sorry about it. Am I going to have to talk to the coppers about this? I don't think I'd be very comfortable with that at the moment."

"You do not. You will not be 'run in' or anything, you were the victim. It's up to you to choose to pursue legal action or report what's happened. Maybe we should switch tracks for a second, eh? How long had you and Nick been together?"

His idea of switching tracks is to go from one painful subject to another, it seems. I don't guess talking about the weather would do me much good.

"About a year. Our relationship was… so natural, you know? We were so comfortable together, like we'd always been with each other." Jarrod was right about that vulnerable thing; just talking about Nick now makes me feel pretty vulnerable. "Maybe it was just me feeling that way, but it seemed so real. I never felt even the slightest doubt that he didn't love me too. I never had any reason to suspect…." I wonder if there's a tube they can put in my throat to keep it from feeling tight like this. "I really loved him," I whisper.

"Did he send you any messages?"

I shake my head and swallow down that painful lump. "He very rarely texted me. Usually rang. There are a few voice messages from him. I didn't… I don't want to listen to him apologizing and hoping we can work things out. Because I would go back. But I can't, can I? Not like this, not after what happened to me. He wouldn't see me the same way anymore."

"Did he ever express anything like that to you? Did he ever have a difficult time dealing with people in a challenging situation?"

"No… I don't guess so."

"Do you think you would want to talk to him again, given the opportunity?"

"Maybe one day. But… not now. I've got too much to work on first. I don't know. In a way, I think so, but…."

"You mean you feel like you want to be in a more firm place, emotionally speaking, before considering that?"

"Yeah."

"Sounds like a good idea. How did he respond when you found him that morning?"

"He didn't, he was asleep. The other guy kind of looked at me like I was a flatmate walking in on them, but I didn't stick around to see much of him. It was dark in there anyway. I don't know, maybe he really did stay here so he could fool around."

"Would he ordinarily have gone along with you and your mates?"

"Yeah, we all hung out a lot."

"What was his reason for not going to Ibiza?"

"His boss wanted him to go to a legal conference here that week. He was a paralegal for the Crown Prosecution in Serious Crimes. Apparently he was brilliant at it, pretty much wrote a few important cases against big crime bosses and stuff."

Jarrod pauses for a moment, doing that "considering" thing again. "What about your friends? How do you think you'd feel if you talked to them again?"

"After what was said in those texts? I don't think they'll want to hear from me again."

"It wasn't you who sent those messages, though. So, how do you think they'd react if they knew that, if they knew it wasn't you saying those things?"

This would mean them knowing who did send them and why…. "I don't know if I could handle that, telling them what happened to me."

"What about it do you think would be difficult for you, in particular?"

That requires a moment of thought and isn't easy to articulate. "I think I'd be ashamed. I don't think they'd say it was my fault, but… they might be freaked out, or really uncomfortable, or… pity me."

Jarrod nods and sits quietly for a moment. "You didn't do anything to be ashamed of, Padrig. I know bad things happened to you, but it's important for you to know that *you* aren't those bad things. And you have the power to overcome your past."

I don't respond. I think I believe him, but it's a bit difficult to realize how much my life has changed. I know I can't just go back to the way things were, but I can't help thinking it might just be a lot easier if I still had my friends. It's very difficult to not have anyone to call a mate.

An unsuppressed yawn sneaks out of me, and I realize how tired I'm feeling again.

"You're wanting a bit of rest, no doubt," Jarrod says and stands up. "I'm glad we were able to talk for a bit, and I'm glad you're making some good steps forward. Don't worry about it all going the right way at once. It takes some time, but I definitely think you can get there. And you're not alone, Padrig, that's the main thing to remember, alright?"

Almost as if he read my mind. I guess he's not a psychologist for nothing. "Alright."

Jarrod reaches out his hand to me, and I take it. "Take care of yourself, Padrig. I'll come round and say hi tomorrow, if that's alright."

"Okay."

"Brilliant. See you then!" He puts his hat back on and waves back to me as he steps out of the room.

I decide to sleep for a while because I have no idea what else I'll do with the rest of the time between now and supper.

CHAPTER 10

IT'S a really lovely spring morning. The sun is bright, and I can hear birds chirping playfully outside. I don't remember hearing birds the whole time I was in that room. Funny thing to notice *not* noticing.

I was allowed some buttered rice for dinner last night and herbal tea. It felt like I really would be on to prime rib and champagne before I knew it. For breakfast this morning I'm having a couple of those puffed rice cakes and applesauce. I now know I'm a fundamentally changed man; I actually don't mind eating the things. I remember one time when Archie had them in (I think his gran had been down to visit for a couple days) and we literally used them as coasters. It all ended poorly when Archie's lager spilled over because the things are so "knobby." *Not* because he was so drunk, of course.

Although I have the sense to stop thinking of good times before that can make me sad, I manage to do something even stupider. I don't know what possesses me to do it. Maybe it's the morning sun, or not being used to having a mostly clear head. Maybe, after all that time, on some deep subconscious level, I'm not comfortable with being comfortable anymore.

I pick up my phone. And turn it on. And think that at some point I'll need a charger for it. Bennett and Alex must have had one. And they must have continued paying my bill, and probably a few other bills of mine, and this is the downside of being able to do everything on your phone—and living with a generous boyfriend. Nobody wanted their bill paid, ergo nobody looked for me.

And then I go to my voice messages, and tap the first one from Nick the day I got home from Ibiza. In that second of suspension between tapping the screen and the message playing, I have a mini-panic attack and think of throwing the phone at the wall so I don't have to hear his voice. I go cold from the chest up, like my heart just can't manage the pressure it takes to get the blood to go upward. I probably take twenty breaths in that single second. And then it's there.

Padrig...? Soft, rasping.

My heart clenches. Why did I do this, why did I think I could handle this? I *didn't* think. There's a long pause.

I.... We.... Shit.

I've never, ever heard Nick at a loss for words. He always knew what to say, even if it took him a moment or two to consider it. And I hardly recognize his voice, but it's not because it's been so long. He sounds like hell. Pretty much like I feel.

Pad, I know... I know you don't want to talk to me. I don't even want to talk to me right now. Just... please, we really *need to talk. Please call me?*

It's been so long, and I just can't listen any longer at the moment. I still love him. The ache, all over, deep and strong and gutting, makes that clear.

Mercy, after everything I've been through, is finally kind to me and lets me go back to sleep for a while on this beautiful morning.

But when I wake up again later in the morning, I can still hear Nick's voice in my mind. As much as I couldn't bear to listen anymore earlier, it's driving me mad now. I've got to hear what else he had to say.

So I pick up my phone and go to the next message from him, the day after I got home. Probably sometime after that first dose of heroin was starting to set in on me.

Pad, baby, please call me. I don't care if you don't want to talk about things, I just need to know you're okay. Frederick keeps telling me he hasn't seen you since he got out of the taxi and he doesn't know where you are. I know you're upset, but please tell me you're alright. *I'm really worried.*

Nick sounds so sad, so… broken. Almost like he knows I'm not alright and he is helpless do to anything about it.

The next one is from a few days later.

I know I don't deserve to hear from you again. I don't blame you. I just wanted a chance to explain, to tell you I'm sorry. I don't know what happened, Pad. I love you, though, I really love you.

The ache surges through me, through all my veins and arteries and along all my nerves and across my *synapses*, for fuck's sake. If I just go to his number and press the little phone icon beside his name…. If we could talk, maybe…. I don't know, maybe he wouldn't care about what happened to me, maybe we could be together again. Does that make me sound pathetic?

I skip over a few of the messages from Nick and go to the one just before Christmas, almost half a year after I went missing. There's a few in between, but they are less frequent as the months pass, and this was the last one from him.

Hi. It's me… again. It's been so long, Pad. I haven't heard anything from you. I don't even know if you will ever hear this. I just….

There's a long pause and a shaky breath.

I'm going… back to New York. For a while. I don't know, I might stay. I can't be here right now. I miss you too much.

Another long, stuttering breath.

I'm so sorry, for everything. I…. I'll call again when I'm settled in, maybe. Or maybe I shouldn't. I don't know. Obviously you don't want to hear from me. I'm sorry, and I don't know if I can forgive myself for losing you. I loved you so much, Padrig….

His voice catches on a sob and breaks when he says my name. The same sob is ripped out of me. If he was here right now, I'd hold onto him and forgive him for everything, no questions asked.

I lie there for a long time, hearing his voice repeat in my mind. Not the broken, ragged voice in those messages, but the one from when things were still good. The one that's soft, with an accent that's faded from years growing up in the States, like a favorite jersey that's been washed so many times. The one from when we used to sit at the kitchen table on Saturday mornings, drinking tea and talking about the weekend's plans. From when we used to curl up on the couch with takeaway and a movie on Fridays after work.

He's gone now though. Maybe it's for the best. I'll never be the same as I was when I was with him. It's probably asking too much to see him again. That part of my life was ended. I can't go backward now anyway. I can only go forward into whatever is waiting for me.

God, I miss him though.

I DON'T eat a whole lot of my lunch, even though there isn't a whole lot to eat. Out of everything I could find to be miserable about, it's missing Nick that's really got me feeling down.

Shortly after lunch, Jarrod comes by to see me. As soon as I see him and his Humphrey Bogart hat, I turn off the telly and push myself upright. Almost before he can get past "hello" I'm ready for him.

"I got to thinking about what you said about that place where I could stay for a while," I say with more determination than I'm quite sure I've got. "Maybe it's not a bad idea, because I don't think I have any place to go from here anyway. And... I just want to get back on my feet again."

"Wanting to is the first step," Jarrod says as he makes himself comfortable in the bedside chair. "If you want, we could go down to Willowmead sometime in the next couple days. Tomorrow even, if you like. That would let you get an idea of whether you think you'd like to stay there for a while. I tend to think you will though."

"Okay, yeah. I think I'd like to go tomorrow, then."

"Brilliant. I'll come around this time, shall I?"

I nod.

"So, how are you doing today, then? You seem rather motivated."

"I guess I am motivated. I listened to some of the voice messages this morning."

"I see." Jarrod sounds like he's trying to not make any assumptions. "How did that go?"

I shrug. "I just picked out a few of the ones from Nick. He seemed dead upset. Though I suppose you would if you'd been caught out and then never heard anything but text messages saying I don't want to talk to you. He did seem worried about me, and like he did love me. He also said he's decided to go back to the States. There weren't any messages from him since then."

Jarrod hums as if he's considering what all that means about Nick. "How did you feel after listening to those?" What a classic question! Maybe he *is* a psychiatrist after all.

"I don't know. On one hand I felt sad about it. I miss him and I know I still love him, despite everything. But in a way, I think it's also made me realize that I can't wait for someone to come along and make things better for me. That's why I want to see about staying at that place. And I want to learn about the medications, even though I'm kind of nervous about that. I just... I want to be in control of my life again, and I don't suppose I can do that if I'm trying to hide from things. I want to get better and I won't let the past rule my future, and I mean to do what I have to do to make sure those things happen."

"I think that's just so, Padrig. Sha-Sha was definitely right about you, you're a hell of a fighter."

I'm not sure what he means by that. Was she annoyed by my questions or not wanting to talk about treatment straight away? She seems to like me though. "Did I say something wrong to her?" I ask Jarrod.

"No, not at all. It's quite a compliment. She just said that she feels like you've got a strong fighting spirit. I believe that as well."

"Oh. I never really thought that about myself. I've always just carried on."

"What have you carried on from before?" Jarrod asks casually.

"I don't know. Not really knowing my parents, I suppose. My mother died just after I was born and my dad died when I was about five. I wasn't related to the woman who raised me, but she was the kindest person I've ever known. She passed away when I was seventeen and I mainly looked after myself from then on."

"I see," Jarrod nods. "How did your da' die?"

"I don't really know. No one ever told me exactly. I asked Aunt Cecily a few times—that's what I called her—and she always just said that he had an illness and wasn't able to recover from it. I guess I never really *wanted* to know the whole story, or just didn't want to press Aunt Cecily about it."

"What do you think you did to help you through that time in your life?"

"Not sure what *I* did. I mean, I was just a kid at the time. But I think having Aunt Cecily helped. She always took care of me while my dad was working when he was still alive, so I guess it wasn't so difficult since there was still someone I was comfortable with there."

"Were you able to talk to her about how you felt, if you missed your dad or were feeling upset about it?"

"Yeah. She had no problem talking with me about stuff like that. I guess she just wasn't very comfortable talking about the dead."

"So that helped, talking about how you felt?"

"I guess so. There were some times when I didn't want to talk, I just wanted to lie in bed and have a cry. I think that was kind of helpful too, though."

"It's definitely alright to just feel your feelings, or to talk about them if you prefer to do that. So, we're on for an outing tomorrow afternoon, are we?"

"Yeah, sure."

"Brilliant. I'm pretty sure you'll like it there. Of course if you don't care for it, that's okay too, we can always look at other options."

"Okay. Um… this is a weird question, but… what am I meant to wear? This is…," I say, plucking at my hospital gown, "not very substantial."

Jarrod looks at me for a moment in confusion and then taps his forehead. "I *am* an eejit. Forgot Geoff was away this week." He walks over to the narrow cupboard in the room and takes out a few garments on hangers. "Geoff is your 'socio-economic advocate'. I'm fairly convinced he's actually a wizard, but. Anything you need, I swear it appears out of nowhere."

"He's got taste," I say, looking at the shirt Jarrod hands me. It's a simple white button-down with blue pin-striping that's so pale and delicately sewn it looks like part of the weave of the poplin. Definitely good quality. He hands me a pair of jeans as well that look so normal and comfortable to wear it almost chokes me up.

"He has, indeed. In other words, you can tell I didn't pick these things. But if you want, we can take a day to go shopping as well. You're bound to need a few more than just what's here, and it's always nice to have things in your own style."

"That would be nice," I agree. "I don't actually… I mean, there's a fiver in my wallet, but I don't know about the rest of my bank account."

"Ah no, nothing to worry about there. You'll see whenever you talk to Geoff, he'll have set up a few things for you temporarily before he left. Telling you, Padrig, the man's a magician."

I'm about to ask more about this guy and what exactly his job entails with regard to my situation, but I'm preempted by a nurse knocking at the door. She says that Dr. Asha mentioned that I could have a short walk around the hospital garden if I was feeling up to it, that it would be good for getting me, quite literally, back on my feet.

"Best thing for it," Jarrod nods. "I'll be round tomorrow, Padrig. If there's anything you need in the meanwhile just give me a ring."

Touring the hospital garden seems like such a big step. I'm curiously grateful that Dr. Asha would think a thing as ordinary as having a stroll outside as something beneficial. It makes me feel like she cares about my overall well-being, not just the medical aspect.

I can't help wondering what it will be like at the center Jarrod and I are visiting tomorrow. He's left a leaflet and it does look nice: a fair-sized Elizabethan manor is pictured on the front. I just hope it's not the sort of place that feels like a small-scale, glorified hospital. I knew a guy in school who had to spend several weeks rehabbing at an old-people's home after being hit by a driver while on his bicycle. I was awkward and uncomfortable the few times some of us went round to see him.

CHAPTER 11

IT TOOK me a few moments to dress yesterday afternoon when the nurse offered to take me out to the garden. I hadn't realized how long it had been since I'd dressed myself, and I admit it was a little emotional. When I came back in from the walk, I was pretty tired out. I remember what it was like after that bout of pneumonia I had as a kid; it took me almost a month to get back to being able to have a kickabout with my mates.

I sat down for a bit then, wishing I could be someplace homely, instead of in a hospital room, and wondering what Willowmead is like. I decided to have a look through the clothes in the little cupboard and I was truly amazed. There are two pairs of jeans and two pairs of chinos, one black and one tan. There are three button-downs, three cotton t-shirts, two jumpers, two sets of pajamas, two belts, a necktie, five pairs of socks, two pairs of boxers and two y-fronts, and two pairs of shoes, trainers and oxfords. Everything is obviously new and as good quality as the shirt Jarrod handed me earlier.

Maybe Jarrod was right about this Geoff guy being a magician.

After having dinner, I decided to take advantage of the little shower in the en suite. I hadn't thought much about how different my body is until then. There was a mirror above the sink and as I took off the button-down I wore for my walk in the garden, I realized just how thin I am. I was always fit, but now I'm kind of scrawny looking. I somehow look older and younger at the same time. Older like I've been through a lot and I'm worn out, younger like I'm underdeveloped and adrift.

At that moment I got the feeling that I've got to remake myself now. I'm going to rebuild my life and I will make sure that my appearance is rebuilt too. In spite of everything, I felt a brief shot of pride. I will want the world to know who I am and what I overcame, eventually.

I'VE had my lunch and I'm just getting dressed when Jarrod comes round to pick me up. At his knock, I open the door. He looks almost surprised to see me up and dressed. I feel that same pride I felt last night, and after a moment I realize that I see the same reflected in Jarrod's expression. He looks proud of me. I can't help pulling him into a hug and whispering, "Thank you."

Jarrod returns the hug and says, "I should be thanking you, Padrig. I can't tell you how glad I am that you're getting up and fighting back."

I didn't know till now how much I missed positive human contact, someone holding me not to keep me down or hurt me, but because they care about me. It's a few long moments before I feel composed enough to pull back from the hug. "I have to at least make a go of it. I think I wanted to give up at first, and I know I might feel like that again sometimes, but just now, I need to try."

"We'll make sure you've got whatever you need to do well," Jarrod says. "And even if you do ever want to quit again, we won't quit you. You don't ever have to be in this alone."

That's probably the nicest thing anyone's ever said to me.

AS JARROD parks his cherry-red Corsa in the private, walled lot, I think that this place isn't at all what I thought it might be. It seems like a secluded resort, the sort of place the rich and famous spend weekends. I don't feel like I'm sitting in the parking lot of a treatment facility at all. The building itself is an Elizabethan country manor. It reminds me of the Littlecote hotel in Wiltshire where Nick took me for my birthday last year. I still don't know how he ever got us a room there, and on a weekend. It's usually booked more than a year in advance.

Stepping out of the car, I try to bring myself back to the present. The grounds are really beautiful, and I think for a moment how wonderful it is to stand, free and clear, in the warm sunlight. There are bright flowers all around, cheery daffodils and a riot of colorful tulips and trees with their little spring leaves on. The apple and cherry trees are in full bloom, and their scent makes me feel happy deep inside. I can see that sectioned-off gardens surround the place and that there are different styles. From here at the front of the house I can see one Asian-style garden off the east wing and a more traditionally English garden at the west wing.

Jarrod leads the way up to the entrance and holds the door for me. The entryway is perfectly in keeping with the outside of the house. It's homely and authentic-looking, from the white walls and exposed beams to the burgundy carpeting and brown leather couches. I still have yet to feel like I'm visiting any sort of convalescent home or bail house—I'm not sure which would be worse.

Jarrod tips his hat to the receptionist as we step in. "Good afternoon, Cordelia. This is Padrig, he's here to have a look about the place. Padrig, this is Cordelia, one of the loveliest, most helpful ladies you could hope to meet."

Cordelia smirks at Jarrod like she's used to his charm, but she stands up behind the desk and reaches over to shake my hand. "Hello, Padrig! So very nice to meet you," she says enthusiastically.

I respond with a comparatively subdued "hi."

"If there's anything you gentlemen need, just let me know," she says. "Marcus checked in earlier today, Jarrod."

"That's good, maybe we'll run into him," Jarrod says.

I wonder who Marcus is and if he's really up to meeting anyone if he's just checked in. Jarrod and Cordelia don't make it sound like he's a patient needing care, but a guest they're glad to see returning.

"Well, Padrig, obviously this is the main lobby," Jarrod says. "If we go straight back from here, there's a big dining room, several smaller meeting rooms, a fitness room. The open kitchen and mini-market is behind the dining room. Through the east wing are the primary medical areas, pharmacy and all that. The west wing is all flats, as are the first and second floors."

Jarrod takes me around to some of the ground-floor facilities. The dining room, obviously once a ballroom, is beautiful. Its style is simple and elegant, somewhat newer than the rest of the house, but it is still natural to the setting. Large, round banquet tables are each set for about ten people and have nice white linens and fresh flowers from the garden.

We look into the open kitchen, which is set up like a cafeteria. Jarrod tells me that you can come down here and pick up fresh food to take back to your flat and do up yourself whenever you like. We also take a short look at the east wing clinic, which maintains some of the original style of the house, but is refitted as a medical area. There are several private exam rooms, a lab area, and the pharmacy. Jarrod tells me that they are able to perform minor procedures there and all.

Over in the west wing, Jarrod shows me one of the long-term flats as well as one of the short-stay rooms. The long-term ones are larger, like a hotel suit, with a living area, dinette-kitchenette, and private bedroom and en suite. The short-term rooms are more like a bedsit or hotel room. They're both comfortably and cleanly furnished and include "all mod cons," according to Jarrod.

"We can have a walk through one of the gardens if you're feeling up to it," Jarrod says as we finish up the indoor tour.

"Maybe we could just sit in the garden?" I suggest. I'm feeling all right, but I've already had a lot of exercise for the day compared to the last few months. Unless being prostituted counts as exercise.

Jarrod shows me the way out to the English garden off the west wing and points out a bench under a gnarly old oak tree that looks like it was planted around the time the house's cornerstone was laid. Honestly, this is one of the nicest places I've ever sat, and the whole place seems really welcoming and comfortable.

Jarrod is starting to mention some of the other amenities and services Willowmead offers when a younger guy, about my age, comes up the path and says hello to Jarrod.

"Hey, Marc! Glad you decided to come. Padrig, this is Marcus, he stays here short-term now and again. Marcus, this is Padrig. I'm just giving him the grand tour."

"Hey, Padrig," Marcus says to me with a little wave.

"Hi," I reply.

Marcus sits down at Jarrod's other side and leans forward to talk to me. "So you're thinking of spending some time here?"

"Yeah." I nod. "I mean, I think. It seems pretty nice."

"It is. I really love it here. I come as often as I can, whenever I need some quiet time. Not just for the meetings, you know? I'm staying for a week right now while my boyfriend is out of town. Didn't want to hang out by myself in the apartment the whole time, even though I'm about fifteen minutes' walk from here. The time I spend here is always really useful for me."

Marcus is so enthusiastic, it's like he's talking about a holiday resort, which I'm not yet convinced this place *isn't*.

Then something occurs to me. "Are you... um.... I'm not sure if it's right to ask this or not. Do you have...." It's not very comfortable trying to say the name of the disease out loud, and I don't want to offend anyone by saying it. It's probably a stupid question anyway, Jarrod said this place is specifically for HIV-positive gay men.

"Oh yeah, I'm positive," Marcus says readily.

"I'm sorry," I say quietly. As the words leave my mouth, I remember that I didn't like it much when those words were said to me.

"Oh, it's okay, I'm not sorry. I know it's a big taboo kind of thing, but I don't hide it. I was a bugchaser, actually."

"A what?" I ask.

"A bugchaser. I intentionally contracted HIV," Marcus explains.

My eyes go wide, and I sort of gasp. "Why would anyone do that?" I say before remembering that I *do* have manners.

Marcus doesn't seem offended though. "All chasers have their reasons," he shrugs. "Some are probably pretty stupid, and a lot of people think they're all stupid, mine included. But I knew what I was doing and I've never not believed in my decision.

"It's kind of a long story, but I lost my partner to an AIDS-related illness, and I made the choice to go through what he went through. I would never advocate that anyone else does that, it's not a normal thing to do, maybe not sane either. But I'm at peace with it. I have no regrets."

I don't respond for a long while; I'm not sure how. I can't imagine *trying* to get sick. I'm still struggling to deal with the fact that I've been diagnosed with HIV, that I didn't make any unsafe choices for myself. I was always careful and took the usual precautions, but I had my choices taken away from me. And here this bloke says he *chose* to get it. And yet, there's something about him that I like a lot, and I find myself wanting to understand his reasoning. I think it's how honest he is about it, but I think in some strange way I can also see how much he must have loved his partner to make a choice like that.

"So, um, you… said you stay here often?" I ask, trying to change the subject a bit.

"Yep. Whenever I feel like I need a break. It's kind of a retreat for me, I can come here and everything is taken care of. I can just relax and take care of me. Don't get me wrong, I love my boyfriend, he's great, but… we're both still *guys*, you know? And he deserves a break from me sometimes too."

"Is he… is he positive, as well?" This is the first I've talked to someone else in my situation. It's one thing to learn about this from Dr. Asha or Jarrod. It's quite something else to be talking to Marcus.

"Oh no, we're a magnetic couple," Marcus says.

"What's that mean?"

"I'm positive, but he's negative. You know, like opposites attract," Marcus says with a grin. "He's not a chaser or anything though, and I'm definitely not a giver. Well, I gotta go get my afternoon doses in a minute."

Marcus stands up and squeezes Jarrod's hand before offering me his. "It was really nice to meet you, Padrig. I hope you do decide to come here, maybe we could hang out. Pretty much everybody here is awesome, but a lot of people out in the world don't want to talk to a former chaser, so it's always nice to meet a friendly person."

"Thank you, Marcus. I really appreciate you talking to me, too."

"Sure thing." He smiles brightly. "See you guys later!"

I'VE done a lot of thinking by the time we get back to my hospital room. The bed has been made up with fresh linens, and on the pillow is a little card. At first I just assume it's a note from a nurse or something and don't think much of it. Instead I start telling Jarrod how nice I think Willowmead is and how I think I'd really like to go there, but I want to sleep on it before I say for sure.

Then I look closer at the card and realize that it's got a picture on it, of a nun I think. On the back there's print in both Cyrillic and English. In English it says:

St. Therese of Lisieux 1873-1897

AIDS sufferers; Australia; aviators; bodily ills; florists; France; illness; loss of parents; missionaries; Russia; tuberculosis

"I'm suffering for only an instant. It's because we think of the past and the future that we become discouraged and fall into despair."

With a questioning look, I hold up the card for Jarrod to see.

"Every so often the clergy comes for a visit," Jarrod shrugs.

THAT evening I'm just finishing my rice pudding dessert when there's a knock at the door. In steps an older fellow, with a very tidy and spry appearance. I almost expect to see a bowler in his hand along with the laptop briefcase he's carrying.

"Good evening, Padrig! I'm so pleased to meet you at last," he says with a ready smile. "I'm Geoffry Moreau, your advocate. Call me Geoff," he says, offering his hand. "I am sorry I haven't been by to see you sooner, but I've been out of town, as I'm sure Jarrod or Asha has informed you."

"Yeah, Jarrod did say so. It's nice to meet you as well." He has a firm but gentle handshake; it makes you think of the sort of person who could politely ask the Queen to let him use Windsor Castle to house a herd of sheep for the winter—and have her jollily agree. Without knowing anything else about him or even what his job entails, I'm already glad he's my advocate.

"We shall have rather a lot of getting to know one another to do, though I certainly don't want to overwhelm you right off. I just wanted to stop as soon as I could and make sure you are set with a few resources. Perhaps we shall have tea later and talk properly. Mind terribly if I sit?"

"Please do." He reminds me of one of my favorite customers from when I worked in Burlington, who always brought me a cup of tea when he came in to have alterations done or to buy a new tie.

"Now then, how are you, my boy? And I really must tell you, I don't care a bit for 'fine' as a response to that question. No one has ever been accurately described as 'fine', in my estimation."

I like him even more. "I'm well enough, I guess. I'll be better when I'm not in hospital anymore."

"I think most anyone would agree to that. Forgive me for having more information about you than you have about me, but I understand that you might be considering taking a residence at Willowmead."

"I am, I think. I went with Jarrod, and I rather liked it there. I guess… I guess I don't really have many other options, but I also don't really know what sort of resources I have just now."

"Ah yes, well there's where I come in. The first thing I can tell you is that your resources are quite secure. It's rather complex and is best kept for another time when we can talk more, but there will be no financial complications to you staying at Willowmead for as long as you'd like. It's all taken care of. Of course, you'll also need some walking-around money, as it were. And for that I have account information for you."

I'm wondering how exactly "it's all taken care of" as Geoff passes to me an accordion folder.

"It seems that you still have active accounts, which, considering the circumstances, you may choose to close. Though it doesn't especially matter if you want to keep them. Either way, you may draw from this account any time you chose for anything at all. The particulars, such as they are, are all included in the information, and of course I'll be happy to answer any questions I can for you. As for necessary items, I do hope the things I brought in for you are satisfactory. Of course, you'll be wanting more than that and, naturally, something of your own style. I would be more than happy to arrange a shopping trip with you whenever you like. I'm thinking the day after you move into Willowmead might be best. Perhaps shopping and lunch?"

What you have to understand about me is that I have never, ever said no to that question. So of everything that has made me feel a little bit better, a little more like *myself*, it's my enthusiastic "yes" to that offer. There is definitely such a thing as retail therapy. Yes, I know that *things* can't truly help, but for now it is kind of a big step for me in feeling in control of my life again.

"Well then, that's settled. Don't forget, now, if you have any questions for me, don't hesitate to ring. My card is in that packet. The main thing is that you're to be focused on staying well, you just leave the fiscal matters to dear old Geoff," he says with a wink. "Now, I really must be off. My partner is waiting downstairs, but I insisted on stopping to see you. Certainly more enjoyable than unpacking any time. Ring me with your moving date and I will see you then, shall I?"

I promise Geoff I'll do just that.

CHAPTER 12

IT'S been one week since I woke up in hospital. One week since I learned I made it away from captivity. One week since I learned I'm HIV positive. Today, I'm moving forward in my life, finally leaving the hospital room and moving into a single, long-term flat at Willowmead.

Jarrod came by this morning to help me pack up my clothes in the case Geoff had brought them in, as well as to help me with the release procedure, before driving me out to Willowmead.

"So how are you feeling about moving in?" he asks as we're on the road.

"I'm bloody glad to be out of hospital, that's for definite," I tell him with a short puff of a laugh. "It's almost a little scary for me, too, though. I don't really know why, I liked Willowmead, I think it'll be a good place to stay."

"Have new situations in general ever been particularly uncomfortable for you before?"

"Not really, I guess. When I was a kid I was kind of outgoing about going new places and meeting new people. You'd think it wouldn't be that way for somebody who lost both their parents so early."

"Everybody processes things differently. It may be that you found reaching out like that to be helpful in healing, which is quite an insightful thing to realize so young."

That sets me thinking for a few moments, mostly about the fact that I have been through a lot of new situations in the last week and that I know I'm going to end up having to sort them out properly. But I don't have to do that all at once, and I don't have to do it all on my own.

And taking care of myself again is going to be both a big step and a big adjustment.

I suppose when it comes down to it, the hospital set-up isn't entirely different from the situation I was in before. I was pretty much stuck to one spare little room the whole time, dependent upon others to do most everything for me—bringing me food, medication, clothing. Now I'll have my own flat to myself; I can cook for myself or go down to the dining room at mealtimes, or even bring in takeaway. It's really something to say that I'll be glad to do my own washing up, especially since that was the one chore I *always* bribed Nick to do. Well, that and the laundry, except that I always insisted on doing the ironing myself.

It's a small place, but very comfortable. I've got a sitting room, bedroom, kitchenette, and combined bath/WC. The furnishings, cookware, flatware, and appliances are all provided and are in good nick. There are linens provided, but I'm thinking of picking up some new ones when I go out with Geoff tomorrow, along with some new, extra-fluffy pillows. What really stands out to me is how clean, fresh, and bright everything is. This place feels like a new start.

I have bi-weekly appointments set up with Dr. Asha down in the west wing clinic for now. She has several patients at Willowmead and keeps an office here as well as at the hospital. She's said that she expects my appointments to be downgraded to monthly after my first month at Willowmead, barring any complications. I'll be talking to her soon about treatment options, but she said the first thing was for me to get settled in my new place.

Jarrod has told me that he's here almost all the time. He does make out-calls, like he did for me in hospital, but the majority of his time is spent at Willowmead. He leads several groups here, including a group session every Thursday evening, which he highly recommends for me. He says that the meeting is for Willowmead residents, long and short term, as well as those who live outside the center, and that partners and friends are always welcome as well.

While I'm moving in—basically setting my one travel bag down and being shown where everything is by Jarrod—the guy I talked with when I toured here, Marcus, comes by to welcome me with a huge gift hamper that takes up my entire kitchenette table. I have to take a moment to fight down tears when he says that it's from everyone at the center and hands me a card signed by all of them. They don't know me at all, but they've all contributed to welcome me?

Marcus offers to hang out with me for a while once everything is sorted and Jarrod heads out to an afternoon appointment. We just talk about general stuff, mostly about what it's like living at the center, what different groups there are, and what is located in the neighborhood.

"Can I brew a pot for us?" Marcus offers.

"Oh, thanks, but I'll get it. You're my guest, right?"

"No formalities, but thanks," Marcus smiles. "It is your first brew up in the new place, though."

"Did you used to live here as well?" I ask from the kitchenette.

"No, I've never lived here full time. I lived with my partner in a flat not far from here and he left it to me when he passed. I do come here a few times a week though. There's the group meeting every Thursday, and I like to come for yoga and sometimes meditation."

I hand Marcus a mug of tea and sit back with mine in the armchair in my sitting room.

"Cheers. So, are you thinking of coming to the meeting after dinner?" Marcus asks.

"I suppose I probably will. Are you going as well?" It might be a little awkward for me going and not knowing anyone other than Jarrod.

"Oh, definitely. I almost never miss a meeting. It's one of the best things in my week," Marcus says. "We can sit together at dinner too, if you want. Or I could run down and bring some food up if you'd rather have dinner here."

"Well, to be honest, I think I kind of would like to eat here. Just for tonight. I'll probably brave the dining room for lunch tomorrow. It would be really nice to share dinner though, if you don't mind."

"Yeah, that's cool, no problem. Just tell me what you feel like having and I'll grab some for us."

They've got some of almost everything down in the kitchen; that way people who have to keep to certain diets don't have to have a special menu or anything. I'm pretty much back to a normal diet after easing into it in hospital. I find that I don't really want to eat a heavy meal though. I always did prefer rather healthy things; it was never a struggle to get me to eat my veggies. And now I think I've somehow decided that swearing off fry-ups and curries is going to help me keep healthy as long as possible.

Marcus brings us up some rice with steamed veg, roasted chicken, fresh bread, a couple bottles of mineral water, and strawberries and cream for afters. It's a really simple meal, but perfectly prepared and almost decadent after eating hospital fare all week. I think I'm really going to enjoy being able to prepare my own food again as well.

It's a bit surprising how easy it is to sit with Marcus, chatting and eating. We only talked for a few minutes when I first came to visit, but Marcus has welcomed me unreservedly and accepted me as if we'd been friends all along. There's a tugging feeling deep in me, a pull that tells me how much I really need a friend at the moment. I miss my old friends as well, and can't help wondering if I'll ever see them again.

And what about Marcus? How would he react to me if he knew my story? Jarrod has said a number of times that I don't have to talk about it, to anyone, unless I feel ready. Really, though, I think I'd rather know upfront if people aren't going to want to be friends with me or are going to be uncomfortable because of what I've been put through.

We've finished dinner and there's still about half an hour before the meeting. As good a time as any to bring this up.

"Marcus... there's something I want to tell you about. I don't know what you're going to say.... I don't know what anybody's going to say."

"Well that's okay, I never quite know what people are going to say when I tell them I was a chaser. I'll always listen, though. What's on your mind, Padrig?"

"It's what happened to me, how I got sick."

"Pad, I don't mean to interrupt, but have you talked to Jarrod about it?"

"Yeah, I have. A few times. I just... wanted to tell you too, because you're pretty much the first friend I've had since it all ended."

"Okay, then. I'm listening."

"It... um. For me it wasn't because I wasn't careful or something. Or maybe it was, in the end." It's so difficult to start, but then I just let it out all at once.

"It's hard for me to think about without thinking that I let it happen or that I could have prevented it or stopped it. I don't know. These two guys... well, one at first. I'd just gotten home from holiday and found my boyfriend in bed with somebody else, and I was sitting there in the park having such a pathetic cry of it, and this guy comes up like he feels sorry for me and offers me tea and someone to talk to. And the next fucking thing I knew, I was drugged and they kept me like that, and hired me out as a rent boy. And I don't know why. I wish I did."

Marcus has come over to sit beside me on the couch and has an arm around me tightly. "It wasn't your fault, Padrig," he says quietly but with determination. "I know it's easy for people to just say things like that, but it's true. I mean, think about it, I'm one person who can unequivocally say it *is* one-hundred percent my fault I'm positive. But for you it's kind of exactly the opposite. And, I know I can't begin to know what you went through, but how could something like that be the victim's fault, Padrig?"

"I don't know. I could have tried harder to get away, but it isn't very easy to think things through when you're high. Or I could have... well, not taken tea from a stranger, for one thing."

"We can't judge ourselves, or each other, based on reactions in vulnerable moments," Marcus says, his arm still around my shoulders. "We always hear about keeping our drinks safe at bars but, come on, tea is supposed to *fix* everything. That's pretty much what I grew up with, anyway."

That gives me one of those watery half-laughs, but it is true. Aunt Cecily used to make me a cup no matter what had happened—failed at maths, sprained ankle playing footie, that time I wore my favorite purple jumper to school and spilt milk on it at lunch.

"It doesn't make you feel weird, being around me, then? Knowing what happened to me?"

Marcus shakes his head. "Does it make you feel weird, being around me, knowing that after my partner died I actively sought HIV-positive men to sleep with, in the hope of seroconverting?"

I honestly do think about it for a second in the way he presents it, but then I say, "No. I won't say I understand why you did that, but I don't feel weird with *you*. You know, who you are."

Marcus nods. "Thanks, Pad. That's kind of how it is, you know. I never expected anybody else to understand, but just to see me as I am, that's all I ask. And that's how I see you too, only you didn't actively do anything 'wrong'."

"Do you think other people will see it that way as well?"

"Some may, some may not. It's almost impossible to predict people. I think I can safely say that anyone you'll meet here won't judge you, though. We've all been through something different and we all know people who have been through some really rough things. I kind of think of this place as a judgment-free zone. It isn't like that everywhere. When I first went for treatment and counseling at a different center, there were a lot of people who wouldn't talk to me. I even had one counselor who tried to tell me it was Jamey's—that was my partner—it was his fault I became a chaser. I booked it outta there after that and started coming here. Couldn't have made a better choice."

"How long has it been for you?"

"Five years since I seroconverted, four and a half I've been coming here."

Five years. I don't think I even expected to live five months after I heard my diagnosis, though I know that was a reaction of the moment. I almost want to ask what it was like for Marcus finding a new partner after losing someone he obviously loved deeply, but I realize that's a little personal, and Marcus is shifting to stand from the couch anyway.

"So, you want to come on down to the meeting with me? We can head down now if you want."

With a breath, I nod and stand as well. "Okay."

"Good," Marcus says with an encouraging smile. "You'll like the guys, and they'll like you. I can almost guarantee it."

CHAPTER
13

I'VE had a lot of positive steps in the last few days, today especially, but I'm still a little shy going into the meeting. I'm glad Marcus is here with me, but it comes to me that there is a whole room of people with whom I have something significant in common. It sort of makes this all… real.

There's a semicircle of about fifteen cushy armchairs and still plenty of space for people to stand about chatting. There are around ten or so people already here, a few seated, some standing in groups. There's also a table along the back wall set up with tea, coffee, water, and little sweets on offer. There's a large sliding door in one wall that lets out to the Asian garden in the east wing of the center. The glass seems to be tinted because it's not quite that dark out, though it did look like rain this evening.

"Looks like Mick is here alone tonight," Marcus says, pointing out a burly bloke who looks like he was probably the one everyone wanted on their rugby team in school. He is sitting off by himself in the circle, not chatting with others, and I have to wonder if he wants to be bothered as Marcus leads me over to him.

"Hey, little M," Mick says as Marcus takes up the chair at his right and I at Marcus's right.

"What's up, big M? Mick, this is my friend Padrig. He's new here, just moved into Willowmead today. Padrig, this is Mick Carlson. He looks all big and scary, but he's really just a teddy bear."

"Ruining my image," Mick pouts before he reaches across for my hand. "Nice to meet you, Padrig."

"Thanks, likewise," I respond, hoping that Marcus is right about the teddy bear thing.

Another man comes up to us and kisses Marcus's cheek. "Sweetheart, isn't one boyfriend enough for you? One's out of town so you find another?" he says with a warm Scottish brogue and a cheeky grin. Before Marcus has a chance to roll his eyes, the slim man with gentle eyes turns and takes my hand. "I'm Allen Cockburn, dear one—and if *that* name doesn't explain it all, what does? How about yourself?"

"Padrig. Kennedy." This is going to take some getting used to, meeting all these people. That was never an issue for me before; I was always the one like Allen, introducing myself first.

"Padrig's new here, Allen," Marcus explains.

"You're very much welcome here," Allen says, still holding my hand and giving it a little extra squeeze before letting go and taking a seat at Mick's other side to chat with him.

People are starting to take seats, and Jarrod, who I saw talking to some other attendees when we came in, moves to a chair at one end of the row. He gives me a smile as if to say he's glad I did decide to come along, and that does help me relax a bit.

Just as it seems he's about to get the meeting started, the double doors at the back of the room are thrust open with dramatic flair. In sashays a tall, thin man with big, beautiful green eyes, full lips, and high cheekbones. He's about my age, in tight black jeans and a shiny black shirt that looks painted on. He might as well be wearing neon brights for the impression he makes.

"Alright, *now* the fun can begin," he says with a distinct lilting German accent.

He's about to swing himself into a chair but stops, looking at me. "*Rekrut?*" he says to himself, then strolls over and holds his hand out to me with a broad smile. I almost hesitate to take it, but when I do, he pulls me up into a hug and kisses my cheek.

"They call me the Berlin Wall, babe, how about—"

"Wall my arse!" Allen snorts. "You'd never stop anybody! *And* you're bloody Bavarian."

"Jealous is cute on you, *Cockburn*."

If not for their grins, and Jarrod's, I'd get the impression that these two hated each other.

"As I was saying, Berlin Wall, but I suppose you would prefer a proper name, so you can call me Krist. Kristof Anders, if you would like. That is not nearly as infamous, though, is it? Pity. Still, I think we are going to be lovely friends, babe." He sits in the free chair beside me. "What do they call you?"

Somehow I recover my wits enough to respond. "Padrig. Pad." I'm not sure why I give him my nickname, or why, despite being a little bowled over, I'm not all that uncomfortable around him. His erratic behavior should have me hiding under the chair by now, but there's something about him that is so... compellingly genuine. I don't see this person ever being anything but utterly honest with me.

"Pad? Ah, that's cute. Suits you perfectly, babe," Krist says, patting my arm. "So, now that we are cozy, what is the agenda for tonight, Dr. Brosie?"

Jarrod's amused smirk says he's used to Krist, and also that he's a complete nutter, but a harmless one. "Well, since Padrig is with us for the first time, I was thinking we could all offer an introduction, perhaps share some of our stories. And if Padrig wants to, he's welcome to share with us too."

Instead of just taking the agenda Jarrod proposes as set, everyone informally gives their agreement.

Marcus starts off, saying, "I don't mind going first, since Padrig and I have already hung out a bit. Anyway, I'm Marcus Smith and I'm positive. I have been for about five years, almost a year after I lost my partner. I'm in a magnetic relationship now. And, um... I was born in California but have lived here in London for about... fifteen years, so, half my life."

"Hello, Padrig. I'm Allen Cockburn and we've just met. So, about me... I'm positive and also lost my partner several years ago. I've been positive for, oh... twelve years, I think it's been? And I'm not in a relationship at the moment. But I'm open to suggestions," he adds with a grin.

"Hi, Padrig. Guess we met too. I'm Mick Carlson. Positive, for three years, and a half. My partner, Oisin, is poz too. He usually attends with me, but he wanted to take it easy tonight. He's, um… not having an easy time adjusting to a new cocktail. Yeah, anyway, from near Devon, and played for Richmond FC for a while."

The group seems to be waiting for Krist to go next, since the first three also had introductions to me when I arrived, but he doesn't. A distinguished, somewhat older man at the other end of the row picks up the thread after a moment.

"Good evening, Padrig. I'm Martin Frisby. I am negative, but I used to attend with my partner, Gier, until his passing a few months ago. And this group has made so much difference in helping me handle everything that I should never be able to thank you all adequately."

Beside him are two who have their chairs pushed together, obviously a couple. One reaches out to touch Martin's arm sympathetically as the other introduces himself. "Hi, Padrig. I'm Clyde. Whitlock, not Barrow," he says. He has an accent that sounds like one of the American Kennedys. "I'm poz, and I've got the most wonderful partner in the world, even if I bitch him out for not letting me get away with missing a dose of meds even one time." Clyde smiles sardonically at his partner, but their hands are clasped like they've never argued a day in their lives.

"I'm Christian Hartford-Whitlock, Padrig. I'm negative, and *I've* got the most wonderful partner in the world, even though he bitches at me for making sure he keeps adherence. I only do it because he's the best of me."

"Shut up, pumpkin," Clyde murmurs affectionately.

There's another momentary pause before Jarrod jumps in. "Well, Pad, we've been working together for a few days now. I guess one of the things I haven't shared with you yet is why I decided to specialize in HIV/AIDS. I was working in psychiatry when I met my first long-term partner. He wasn't diagnosed until around late-stage in progression, and it was too much for him. He just didn't feel he had the heart to fight it. After he died, I felt I needed to do more to understand and to help others in that situation."

"So, want to take a turn, Pad?" he says.

Taking a long breath and exhaling slowly, I shift in my chair and sit up straighter. "Okay. Um... so, I'm Padrig, Padrig Kennedy. I grew up in East London... still here, obviously. I lost both my parents pretty early, lived on my own since I was seventeen. Worked in a shop down in Burlington Arcade until a couple years ago." It's about that point when I realize that I'm not really talking about *myself*. I take another breath and sort of pull my knee up to my chest, an old habit of mine when feeling uncomfortable.

"I, um... only just found out I'm positive last week. I was in hospital because.... I spent several months being drugged and prostituted involuntarily. And, that's why I'm here."

Marcus reaches over to squeeze my hand and a few of the guys get up to offer hugs, thanks for sharing something difficult, and reassurances of safety and welcome here. I know I didn't exactly give them all the details, but just getting it out, saying it out loud in a group—what I was most worried about—is relieving. I really am moving forward in my life, and though I've certainly got a lot to deal with still, I'm more confident than ever that taking one step at a time will get me there. Wherever there is.

Jarrod seems like he's ready to introduce a new topic for discussion, but then Krist leans forward.

"Everyone here knows I have never really said much about my situation," Krist says in a tone that I gather is dead quiet for a bloke like him. "My standard line has always been 'I'm poison, deal with it.' But after hearing what Pad shared, I think I should share how I got here as well."

Jarrod looks slightly surprised but nods to encourage him to continue. Krist doesn't catch Jarrod's nod, but I don't imagine he needs it. He turns to me and looks me in the eye.

"You are not alone, Padrig. I know what you have gone through."

He takes my hand and continues. Anyone else hearing what he has to say is purely incidental because he is talking directly to me. "I was in the *Bundeswehr*, army, and we were sent into combat in the

Middle East. We were there only a few days before I got separated from my troop after a roadside attack. I was taken by the opposition. I was there seven months. Have no fucking idea what they tried out on me, all manner of drugs. A lot of time they spent practicing how to rape on me. I have no memory of being rescued, just one day waking up in base camp and being transported home. Nobody talked to me about it. I spent weeks in hospital, had every fucking test done on me. And then I was given an HIV-positive diagnosis and discharge by the prick who was my commanding officer, and who I am still not convinced did not 'lose' me purposely out there.

"Now then," he says, looking away from me and around to the others, "that is not to leave this circle, ever. According to the German government it never happened, but Padrig deserves to know that he is not the only one."

Everyone in the room looks gobsmacked, but I pull Krist into a tight hug and thank him. Krist kisses my damp cheek and squeezes my shoulders. "I move we adjourn early," he says to Jarrod.

THAT night, I'm lying in bed in my new flat for the first time. I've left the window open a bit, enough to let me hear the rain shower outside and its steadfast "shhhh." Drops off the overhang tap out an irregular mantra as I snuggle into the pillows and try to wait for sleep.

I've been thinking for a while about what Krist shared and how rare it must have been for him to tell that to anyone. I don't know if he'll want to, but I think I'd like to talk to him more about our similar experiences. Maybe I should ask Jarrod if it would be a good idea. Maybe.

I'm just about to fall asleep when I remember what this moment reminds me of—the only birthday I got to share with Nick, when he took me to Littlecote for the weekend. The bed was just this feathery-soft, and it was rainy that night. I remember the feel of Nick spooned up behind me, his arm tucked around my waist, him whispering, "I love you, Pad."

I think if I was given one wish, to live without HIV or to have Nick back... I'd take Nick.

CHAPTER 14

MY FIRST few days at Willowmead are busy. As promised, Geoff comes round to see me the day after I moved in and offers to take me over to South Leigh, the high street here.

"Do you think you should prefer to walk over? I've parked there, but I can certainly bring the car round. It's not far, just two blocks down from here and across the park, which is a very nice walk on a day like this. It depends on if you're feeling up to it, of course."

Up to it? I'm gagging for a walk! "Actually, I think that would be perfect, having a walk over. I might not be as keen about carrying things back over though."

"No, I think not. We'll drive back over for certain. I'm sure you'll have plenty of packages by the time we're through."

Geoff wasn't half wrong about that. I had tried to take it easy with the shopping, but Geoff kept pointing me toward top quality and insisting that money really was no object. By the time we take a break for lunch at a café, there's several hundred pounds worth of bed and bath linens, including a couple of pillows that I can hardly wait to try out tonight.

Over celery soup and frisée salad, and a really nice pot of Darjeeling, I attempt to ask Geoff once again if it's really okay for me to be spending like this.

He leans back slightly in the metal bistro chair. "You really must trust me on this, Padrig. Everything will be taken care of; you have nothing to worry over. Now, if you want to buy a house or a yacht, you might want to let me know, but I wouldn't rule those out either. There will be more time for me to explain it all later, but for now, let's just enjoy this lovely afternoon, shall we?"

I can't help the feeling that something is being kept from me, but neither do I feel there's any underhanded or malicious intention behind it. I just don't quite understand this concept of being given room and board in a very nice facility *and* being told that I have essentially unlimited funds. It's all a little *Harry Potter* to me. Then again, Geoff's suggestion of enjoying the afternoon is a sound one, and in the warm spring sun, I can easily let the matter go until some other time.

After lunch, Geoff directs me to the clothes shops. I somehow manage to keep that in check, compared to the linens, mostly because I don't feel as though I need a lot of things. I'm also starting to feel a bit tired and am grateful that Geoff can tell as he suggests I can come over to do more shopping any time I fancy.

THAT evening after dinner, Krist comes round to my flat to help me sort out all the bags I've brought back.

"I'm supposed to have an appointment with Dr. Asha tomorrow, to talk about my treatment options." I mention as I'm dividing the white linens from the dark for washing. "How did you deal with that? I mean, only a week ago I was hoping I'd never see drugs again, you know?" I'm not sure how many other people would understand what it's like to have been drugged for so long, only to find out that you've got to take more drugs to stay well.

"I chose not to deal with it at all," Krist says. "My first treatment, it was horrible. I had never been so sick, for months."

"You didn't try another treatment?"

"No. I decided after that experience that I had enough decisions taken from me and I was going to live life as I chose. Doing everything with a big fucking bang, Pad-babe."

"Krist… you don't take anything, at all?" I ask, moving to sit on my couch.

"I do, I take my chances," Krist grins, sitting beside me. Then he wraps an arm around my shoulders and pulls me close. "Ah, Pad-babe, I dislike seeing you worried. I do what I want, you know? I live my life as I see fit. I drink what I want, eat what I want, and I do *other* things as I want as well. I live hard, Pad, no secret to that. I *live* well. *Being* well is another story."

"I'm just the opposite," I murmur. "I want to be healthy for as long as I can."

"You should, you should! Pad-babe, I do not mean anybody should live like me—positive or otherwise. But it is how is right for me. You understand how it is." Krist strokes a hand over my hair.

"I guess," I reply, but I'm not really sure I do.

"You know who would be a good influence for you? Little Marcus. He is very serious about being healthy. I think it drives his boyfriend a bit mad at times."

"Krist, I have to tell you, you and Marc have been really good friends to me in just these last couple of days. It's really made things a lot better, just having a couple of mates again."

"I know, babe," Krist says, kissing my forehead.

THE next morning at breakfast, Marcus waves me over to his table after I've gathered a plate from the buffet.

"Hey, Marc, I wanted to ask you about something. I almost hate to ask first thing at breakfast, but—"

Marc passes packets of butter and black currant jam to me and says, "Nah, don't even think about it, ask me anything."

Buttering my toast and trying to sound casual, I say, "Well, I'm supposed to have an appointment in a couple hours with Dr. Asha to talk about treatments. If you have a few minutes to spare, do you think you'd mind coming with?"

"Sure thing, I'd be more than happy to."

"Really? You wouldn't mind?"

"Not at all. My partner's coming to pick me up later in the afternoon, but I'm free all morning."

"Ok, ta. How's it been for you, with the medication? If you don't mind me asking."

"Not too bad. The first couple months were a little challenging. But after a while you get better at managing the side effects and then they go away. Or they did for me. Everybody's a little different, of course. Once I was past that, I pretty much haven't had any issues at all."

He and Krist really are kind of polar opposites. It goes to show that no matter how much information I had, there is no substitute for talking with those who have been there.

Marcus's support is really helpful during my appointment. It's not even so much his advice or encouragement, or offers to help with keeping me on schedule. It's just the fact that I have a friend to come and sit with me. Not having to be there alone while contemplating what medications I'm going to have to take, and what sort of side effects I'm likely to deal with, makes me feel a lot better.

On Dr. Asha's recommendations, I'm to start treatment Monday. I'll have another appointment with her early in the day, and she will go over the treatment regimen in detail with me then. I reckon I'll probably need some support at first, at least until I'm used to this.

I know it's not the same as the drugs that were forced on me before, but I'm still a little uncomfortable with the idea of taking things. There are some things in my life that I know are never going to be the same. I used to smoke occasionally, and I was a moderate drinker. At the moment, I don't really know if I ever want to drink again and there's no way I'm going back to the fags—that's right out.

After the appointment, Marcus invites me back up to his room for lunch. He says he could use a hand packing up as well. I really appreciate his unspoken offer to distract me from dwelling on this medical stuff, though I guess I'll have time for that once his boyfriend picks him up.

"So what are you doing tonight?" Marcus asks as we're finishing off the lunch that he's had delivered up to the room. "I just ask because you could always come over to our place for dinner, if you're not planning anything."

"Thanks, mate, but I couldn't do that. Your boyfriend just getting home, you don't want a third wheel. I'll probably invite Krist round for afters; he seems to be something of a professional distraction."

Marcus grins slightly. "I didn't mean to be obvious, but in all honesty, yeah, I was thinking you could probably do with company. You really wouldn't be a third wheel and you *are* welcome to join us for dinner, or anything else, any time, Padrig. I know how valuable it is having friends who accept you."

"Thanks, Marc. I'm seeing how valuable they are as well." I just wish I knew if my old friends would be in that category.

"I can come by Monday too, if you want somebody to come with you for your appointment then," Marc offers as he starts taking clothes out of the drawers and putting them into his travel bag.

"I appreciate that, but like I said, your boyfriend just got home... you don't have to—"

Marcus stops what he's doing and turns to me. "Stop being polite, Padrig. Listen, I understand this can be a scary time. I promise I won't be doing this 'mother hen' thing all the time, and if you really think you're okay with it, that's great too. But don't be afraid to accept or ask for help, especially early on. That's why we're here, Pad. Everybody at Willowmead. We all support one another."

It takes me a few moments to respond because I've got to swallow past an annoying lump of emotion in my throat first. "Thank you, Marc. And yeah, maybe I could do with a mate at my appointment. And as far as mates go, you're probably the best one for the job."

"Attaboy," Marc smiles, reaching over to squeeze my shoulder. "Besides, I can stay for yoga hour after lunch, you can come with if you want."

"Okay."

"Would you mind getting my stuff out of the closet while I grab my shampoo and stuff in the bath? Just toss 'em in the bag, doesn't have to be neat."

"Yeah, no problem." Of course, I fully intend to keep whatever's in there folded and tidy, regardless of what he says about "tossing 'em in."

There's a knock at the open door as someone steps in and says, "All set, babe?"

Hearing that voice, my head whips around from the open closet, and I just stare.

CHAPTER 15

"YEAH, just about," Marcus calls from inside the bathroom.

For a moment I can't speak. There's no way that's.... "Freddie?" I half gasp, half ask, the wind knocked out of me.

Freddie looks toward the closet across the room. His eyes narrow and brows furrow momentarily as if he's trying to place me, then they go wide and his jaw drops. "Jesus motherfucking Christ," he breathes.

"Hey, Freddie. I want you to meet my friend, Padrig," Marcus's voice echoes around the tiny bath over the whinge of drawers being opened. He's completely unaware of Fred and me staring at one another like we've both seen ghosts.

Freddie takes a few steps toward me, scrutinizing me in a once-over. I try to brace myself for the confrontation that, considering the text messages on my mobile, seems inevitable. But then Fred pulls me into a long, fierce hug.

"Where the fuck have you been, Kennedy?" His voice beside my ear is rough. Then suddenly he pulls back and stares. "Why are you *here*?"

"You guys know each other?" Marcus asks, surprised to come out of the bath to see Freddie hugging me like long-lost brother.

I'm still speechless.

Freddie looks back and says, "You know I told you about that mate of mine who went missing a couple months before we met?" He steps back and sits down heavily on the bed. "God, Padrig. What the hell happened? Last thing I heard you'd decided you didn't want anything to do with any of your mates anymore. I understood it at first that you just wanted some time alone, finding out about Nick like that... but why did you think we'd helped him with it, man?"

I'm glad of the wing chair beside the bed; I need to sit. "It's a really long story," I say, though talking isn't easy at the moment.

"Hey, Pad," Marcus says gently, sitting beside Freddie but reaching out to me. "You don't have to if you aren't ready."

"I think I need to, Marc. Freddie and I were really good mates, for a long time."

"Ok. Just don't rush, okay?" Marcus squeezes my hand, and I notice how worried Freddie looks.

"This is to do with Nick, isn't it?" Fred asks quietly. "He was messing around and got you sick. Padrig, that's illegal, he can't—"

"Frederick," Marcus warns sternly.

"It's okay, Marc. I... honestly, I'd thought of that at first, even if I wouldn't admit it to myself, but... we *always* used condoms for anything, you know, like that. And considering the circumstances, it's much more likely to have been.... Fred, this isn't easy."

"What happened, Pad? Please tell me. And no, I don't mean to push," he says, pre-empting Marcus, "but... we were mates. I don't understand."

After taking a couple deep breaths, I think I can talk about this. It's not the same as talking about it with someone who doesn't know me—or rather, didn't know me before. This is something else again. Freddie knew me, and we *were* mates, best mates. I cared a lot about him, and I hate telling him something that will hurt him to hear. Or is that just what my ego puts up to deflect the discomfort of having to think about it again?

"It happened that morning, right after we got back from Ibiza. I came in and Nick was asleep in bed with some other guy."

"Fuckin' A. I always reckoned you two for couple-of-the-year. And him for boyfriend-of-the-year, I thought he fuckin' adored you, man."

Yeah. Me too.

"I guess I could understand that you'd blame just about anybody." Freddie says apprehensively.

"I didn't, though. I never for a second thought anything like that. I *was* going to ask to stay with you. I never sent any of the messages you had after we got back, I never blamed you lot or said those things about you. What happened was that...." This requires a deep breath.

"Some guy saw me down the park having a cry and took me back to his for tea. Only I didn't get out of there for months. It was him and another guy. I was... pretty heavily doped up most of the time, and... um...."

Funny that it's the drug thing that I'm most anxious about when talking about treatment, but I find it really difficult to verbalize the sexual side of it all. I think "assault" is the word I'm most comfortable using, but it's not quite accurate either.

"I woke up in hospital maybe a week and a half ago."

Freddie is silent for a long while, just looking at me in incomprehension. I'm not sure if he doesn't believe me or just doesn't know what to say.

"Pad...," he says eventually. His voice is rough again. "Jesus, Padrig. I never knew... I never had any idea. I... I don't know what to say; I feel so fucking guilty."

"You didn't do anything to be guilty about," I tell him quietly.

"Fuck, Pad. I should have known something wasn't right. I was fucked off about it, I should have been worried about you."

"Please don't blame yourself," I all but beg him. "You couldn't have known." The last thing I want is anyone feeling hurt because of what I went through. That is nearly as bad, maybe even worse than someone rejecting me for it.

"No, I fucking blame *Phillip Nicholas*, screwing around on you," Fred says bitterly as he swipes tears out of his eyes.

"Um... yeah, I know, but...."

Fred gets up and pulls me up into another long hug. "Look, why don't you come home with us, okay? We can all have some dinner, and I think we've got a lot of talking to do. I'm not losing my best mate again."

Marcus stands up and puts a hand on Fred's shoulder. "You're welcome to join us, Pad, I told you that earlier."

I'd forgotten about Marc inviting me over to distract me from thinking about starting treatment in two days. Guess I've got the distraction sorted after all.

"Okay, yeah."

CHAPTER 16

FOR a long time I didn't expect I'd ever see my friends again. Then I spent nearly all my time in hospital wondering if they would still want to know me if they knew what had happened. After only a couple days living at Willowmead, I've been happy to make new friends and have started to realize that anyone who wouldn't accept me because of what I've been through couldn't be counted as a friend anyway.

And suddenly my best mate shows up, picking up his boyfriend, one of my new friends, at Willowmead. My life seems to be a series of jarring fits and starts.

Marcus had mentioned that their place was near Willowmead. Very near, in fact, only a block away from the high street where Geoff took me yesterday. It's quite a nice flat on the second floor of a well-preserved building. The place is a lot more spacious than I'd have expected, and Marcus tells me that his partner James bought adjoining flats and had them renovated into one.

I can't help but compare it to the tiny one Freddie and Archie used to share. The place was so crowded with their tottering towers of videos and CDs, and clothes everywhere, as to be nearly impassable. Archie always used to say that there were in fact pathways through the flat, but that you needed a map to find them. This place, though, is tidy and comfortable and gives a very healthful impression, especially when Marcus opens the doors to the cozy balcony. Marcus must be a good influence on Freddie.

Marcus decides he's going to fix us something to eat and tells Freddie and me to hang out and catch up. Freddie offers me something to drink. He pauses for a moment when I turn down the lager in favor of plain water. I don't guess he's ever heard that from me before.

Freddie hands me a bottle of water from some tropical island and gestures to the lounge. A year ago the gesture would have been silly on his part, completely unnecessary. We were at home in one another's homes.

"So, what's been… going on?" I ask, sitting on the sofa and glancing around. Freddie's World War II posters—exhorting British women to "Join the ATS" and telling everyone that *their* courage, *their* cheerfulness, and *their* resolution "will bring us victory"—remind me that I am, in fact, sitting with my best mate.

"Not much different, I guess. I live here with Marc now, obviously, but still working for The Old Lady. Archie is still buying for Harrods. He's away for a few weeks on a buying trip at the moment."

Freddie does some accountant or actuary kind of thing for Bank of England. I suck at maths and have never wanted to know what he does, exactly. It would make my head throb just hearing about it, I'm sure. Archie's work was something I understood a lot better, both of us being in menswear. Only he was always more involved in high fashion, whereas I worked in very traditional apparel.

"I'd love to see Archie again," I say almost to myself. "Is he still angry with me?"

"Oh no, he never was, not really. I hate to say it now, but we disagreed on that and I… well, I nearly stopped talking to him. Marc really had a go at me about that though. He's way too good at that tough love thing."

I can't help but grin. "I'm glad you found Marc, he's a lot smarter than you are."

"Oi! I'll do you for that!" Freddie cries and comes at me menacingly.

I squeak and try to scramble away, but Freddie locks his arms around my waist and drags me back down to the sofa. We're cackling like fools as Marcus looks around the doorway from the kitchen. He just shakes his head and goes back to cooking.

Freddie eases up but keeps an arm around my shoulders as we sit back, laughing and trying to catch our breath.

"I missed you, Pad. Things weren't at all the same without you around," Fred says.

"I missed you all as well. I mean, I missed fucking everything, pretty much, but one of the first things I thought of in hospital was could I ever talk to my mates again. I know it sounds bad, but after everything, I wasn't sure anyone I knew would be comfortable around me anymore."

"I can understand feeling that way, especially since I was a little brutal in those texts. But you had to know I'd never... we'd never.... It wasn't like it was your fault." Freddie stops and sighs; he never was eloquent. "That's not what I'm trying to say. I think my anger in those messages was just... my way of hiding how much it hurt not having you around, or not admitting to myself that I was worried. And I'll tell you, you're right about Marc being good for me. I've learned a hell of a lot about life and how to deal with things from him. I mean, I admit it's going to take me a little while to get it through my thick head, or I guess I mean to process it, that you've been through a really tough time. Right now I'm just fucking amazed you're back. What are the odds you'd end up hanging out with Marc, you know?"

I nod, and we're quiet for a few moments.

"How long is it you've been at Willowmead now?" Freddie asks after a while.

"Just a couple of days. I came right in from hospital after they kept me around for observation. I really think they just wanted to make sure I had a good place to go to."

"Then you're only just.... Wow. Do they know how long you've been positive? I mean, if you want to talk about it. I understand if not."

"It's okay." I shrug. "I don't guess it's known for sure, but it doesn't seem like it happened long after... um, after I was taken."

I think I'm beginning to feel inured to talking about this, but I'm not sure that's a good thing. It feels like I'm skipping steps. The day I moved into Willowmead, though, Jarrod and I discussed stages of trauma, and he said one thing to keep in mind is that there is no timetable or set plan for them, and some people experience them out of order.

"I'm meant to be starting on treatment Monday," I mention to Freddie, hoping to change the subject. "To be honest, I'm a bit nervous about it. I've heard the medication can be really tough to take."

"Who's your doctor?" he asks, probably just as eager to talk about something other than what I went through.

"Dr. Sharma-Penston."

"She's Marc's as well, Dr. Asha, and she does my tests. I think she's one of the best in this country. I know everybody has a different experience with the meds, but you're really in the best hands, she'll do anything she can for you. And so will we, Marc and I."

"What tests do you have?" I ask with a frown. I thought Marcus had said his boyfriend was negative, and….

"I get quick tested every three months, whenever Marc goes in to have all his levels checked. We're as safe as possible, but there's no excuse for not getting tested. And Marc told me the first time we went out that once we start sleeping together I'm getting tested every time he does or we're done."

"You… you mean you…. You, um…."

"Have sex?" Freddie grins. "Yeah. Frequently."

"Oh. Isn't that…. I guess I never thought…."

"It's down to individuals to decide if they still want to. I mean, if you think about it, pretty much everybody uses protection anyway, so honestly it's not all that different. We're just a little extra careful."

"Hey you two, come and eat," Marcus calls from the dining room table.

Marcus has the world's best timing!

"Missed your cooking, babe," Freddie says and kisses Marcus's cheek as we sit down at the table.

"Well, I've missed something too." Marcus winks just before Freddie yelps.

I can't help snickering and hope I'm not blushing much. "This all looks wonderful, Marc," I tell him. There are veggies, brown rice and black beans, hummus and wheat flatbread.

"Thanks," Marcus says. "It's just what we had around. I'll have to go grocery shopping tomorrow afternoon."

"Nah, don't let him fool you," Freddie says. "He jars this veggie salad stuff himself, and mashes up the hummus as well."

"It takes, like, literally, five minutes to make fresh hummus," Marcus shrugs. "And the 'veggie salad stuff' is called *escabeche*. It's just pickled vegetables. Kind of like a Mexican version of Italian *giardiniera*, only not spicy. I grew up snacking on this stuff in Cali. My folks ran a few different restaurants, I just paid attention when people were working."

Marcus might be modest about it, but Freddie is right and everything is delicious. I notice a lot of photos on the dining room wall. Most of them are of Marcus and another bloke holding one another close and looking like... well, looking as happy as I always thought Nick and I were.

Marcus must have noticed me looking because he gets up and takes one off the wall to show me. "That's me and Jamey," he says fondly.

Jamey looks a lot like Marcus: they both have the same dark hair and bright blue eyes, though Jamey is more pale and thinner with more pronounced features. They're in front of a big old castle and Jamey is wearing a formal kilt, so I'm guessing they're in Scotland. I briefly glance over at Freddie, wondering if he's okay with Marc talking about his old partner.

"Oh, it's cool," Freddie says, reading my glance like he always could do. "I'm not here to *replace* James in Marc's life." He reaches over and hold's Marcus's hand, giving him a smile.

"Jamey was just starting to have problems when this was taken," Marcus says. "He died about six months after. I guess it was fast. In one way it felt too fast, but it was also way too slow. What he had was so difficult to deal with, something called PML. It kind of made it seem like he was drunk all the time—he had a tough time seeing, couldn't talk well at times, balance was hard for him. He went into a coma at the end."

"I'm sorry to hear that," I tell him softly, handing the photo back.

"Thanks," Marcus says to me. I see Freddie squeeze his hand supportively as Marcus brings their clasped hands up to his lips before he gets up to put the photo back.

MARCUS and Freddie offer me their guest room to stay for the night if I want, but I prefer coming back to my own place at Willowmead. Freddie offers me a drive back over and walks up to the flat with me to have a look in at the place. As he's going, he wraps me up in a big hug and says, "I'm fucking glad you're back, Pad."

"I'm glad too, Fred. And I'm glad for you and Marc as well. Just… please be careful, okay?"

"Sure thing, Padrig." He winks, then adds, "And you make sure to take care of yourself, all right? Anything you need, let us know, mate. We're here for you. Even if you just want to hang out, any time. It's always been that way and nothing's changed."

Lying in bed later, I can't help thinking of how comfortable Freddie and Marc are, and how happy Marc and James looked in the photos, despite their challenges. I close my eyes and try to remember what it was like, having someone in bed beside me, holding on to me. Someone to kiss me when I was feeling down. Someone to bring me a cup of tea in the morning. Someone to tell me I'm beautiful when I've got a cold and am feeling like absolute rubbish.

I wish so hard I could shake the feeling I'm never going to have that in my life again, the one thing that always meant the most.

CHAPTER 17

MONDAY is kind of a weird day for me. Marcus came round first thing in the morning and shared breakfast with me, even though I wasn't feeling very hungry and just nibbled at the fruit salad he brought, and made some toast and tea for us both. This is supposed to be the "easy" appointment. I've already done the one where it's decided what I'm going to take; this is just meant to be going over the regimen and receiving the actual pills. I guess that's the scary part for me, though. Once I have them and start taking them, I kind of can't go back. I can no longer let myself think that because I can't feel it, it isn't there.

Once again, Marcus's presence and encouragement at my appointment is appreciated. He's offered to do so much to help me through these first few weeks—everything from offering to ring and remind me about taking meds on time, to helping me sort out a gentle but nutritious menu in case I get any digestive side effects, to showing me some relaxation methods to help get through it all.

To get a jump on the last one, Marcus introduces me to the yoga group after we had a bit of lunch. It's held in the same room as the group meeting on Thursday evening, but the chairs have been pushed back against the walls. A comfortable breeze is let in from the doors letting out to the garden, but the vertical shades on the doors are drawn and left half open so the natural light is low. The wall lights around the room are left on dim as well.

A few people are already here and setting up their mats in a wide circle; they were all at the group meeting my first night here—Jarrod, who seems like he's leading this group as well; Mick, the big rugby bloke; Allen "if that doesn't explain it" Cockburn; and Clyde who was there with his partner on Thursday. I'm almost surprised to see Clyde without Christian; even though I only met them the once, they gave that immediate impression of a couple who does everything together and are almost annoyingly happy about it. "You can't have one without the other," as Sinatra said.

Marcus has brought his own mat, but he said there's always a few extra available for anyone to use, so I grab one of the ones in the corner and join in. Jarrod claps my shoulder as he passes me on the way to his mat that's already set up and asks if everybody's ready.

I never really did actual yoga before. I used to go to the gym a few days a week and I made sure to stretch regularly before and after. Some of the moves are challenging enough to figure out how to get into them, let alone trying to hold them for any length of time. Being a beginner isn't so bad though, and there's no pressure to be proficient all at once. And if nothing else, I was definitely good for the part at the end where we just lie there still for about ten minutes.

Returning my mat after the session, I notice that Mick packed up his mat and water bottle quickly and only said a few words to Jarrod before hurrying out. He seemed like he was having a tough time getting into some of the moves through the session too, and I wondered if it was his first go as well. I'm about to ask, but then Marcus invites me over to have dinner with him and Freddie again that night, and tells me there's no way I'm allowed to say anything about third wheels now that he knows Freddie and I are old friends.

We walk back over to his through the park, the same way Geoff and I had gone to South Leigh a few days ago. "You know, there's something I want to mention to you, but I'm almost not sure if I should," Marcus says, measuring his words. "Not that it's anything bad or offensive, just… well, it's something that I never really told Freddie and I hope it wouldn't make you feel uncomfortable. I know how he is at sharing things though—feelings, I mean, not opinions—and it's just my observation anyway…."

"Or you could just tell me whatever it is," I say with a half grin.

"Yeah, I know I can be heavy on the disclaimers. I used to be a Californian, remember?" Marcus smirks. "Anyway, it's just that

Freddie would probably never say it, or even admit to himself, but when we first met I could tell there was something sort of 'lost' about him, you know? I almost hesitated to start dating him right away because I kind of thought he'd just gotten out of a long relationship. Until he told me that he had never *had* a long relationship and it was a fight he'd had with a close friend. Pad, I just have to tell you, he hasn't stopped talking about you since Saturday night. He's really glad you're back."

"Yeah, Freddie probably wouldn't admit he was 'lost' without me," I say with a nostalgic chuckle, thinking of how many times we'd gotten hopelessly lost driving down to the coast over the years. "I wonder if it's hit him yet that I'm positive and that it wasn't really me he was fighting with all that time."

Marcus puts an arm around my shoulders. I guess he sensed my changed tone, but I'm a little surprised with myself by how the words "I'm positive" slipped out without even a mental stutter. "I can't say about the situation you were in, but one thing I can tell you is that Freddie isn't serophobic. In fact, he's pretty passionate about that."

"Serophobic? Is that like people who are afraid of positive people?"

"Yeah, pretty much. It's not as bad as it was back in the eighties and nineties, but there's still enough of it. I've had even nurses and doctors who recoiled when I told them I'm HIV positive, and I told you about that therapist I saw before coming to Willowmead. Personal reactions are bad enough, I don't even want to talk about the legislated serophobia. Unless you want to know, of course. Knowledge is power."

"No, I think I could put off that knowledge, for a while at least."

"Good. Let's focus on positive things. Sorry, sero-joke."

I actually find myself laughing at that, probably just because it's Marcus saying it and his openness is irresistible. He's the sort who turns the light on the monster in the closet and shows it was just a cat who got stuck in there all day.

"How did you two meet anyway?"

"At a London Pride thing last year. I saw him walking around with Archie a couple times, figured they were together and I was just looking anyway, but then I caught him looking back. We did that simultaneous shy smile thing, and next thing I knew he's walking over to chat me up. Said I was the cutest guy he's ever seen."

"That's a shite pick-up line! I mean, you *are* cute and all, but... there's no originality in that, is there?"

"Yeah, I know. And I laughed when he used it on me. But I figured I'd give him a whirl, and that I'd kind of rather hear a dull line like that from a guy who's nice as well as hot, than a clever line from a jerk."

"Good point. Some guys can talk a good game. Better one who *plays* a good game."

"Pretty sure nobody's ever accused Freddie of talking one," Marcus chuckles. "He makes me happy though."

"I've known him for a long time, I think you make him pretty fucking happy too, mate."

AFTER hanging out with Marcus and Freddie, they both ride me back over to Willowmead. Marcus said he came to help me with taking my meds for the first time, which basically meant holding my hand. He said not to hesitate to ring and talk to him about any side effects, even if it's three in the morning.

Swallowing those pills is the most difficult thing I've ever done. It's like taking cyanide capsules for the part of me that was hoping to use the "ignore it and it will go away" strategy indefinitely. I try doing it like it's nothing, just taking some vitamins or a couple pain pills. I double-check that I have the right pills and the right amount of them before popping them in my mouth and swallowing down with a big drink of water. And then I have a minor panic attack. What if I find out that test was wrong and I'm really fine. Would these pills mess up something in me permanently?

Freddie is in my sitting room, but Marcus is right beside me in the kitchenette. After a moment, he puts his hand on my shoulder and says, "I know that took a lot of courage, Pad."

"I just wonder how much the rest of this is going to take." I hate how shaky my voice sounds.

"I won't lie, it takes a lot of courage. But just don't forget, you aren't alone, you don't have to have all the courage all the time."

"You lot are going to get dead sick of filling in my courage when I'm ringing you at two in the morning whinging about being sick to my stomach," I say, accepting Marcus's hug.

"Won't be any worse than your whinging about having a hangover every morning in Ibiza," Freddie says, walking in and making it a group hug. "Told you, mate, anything you need, we're here. Full stop."

"Thanks, guys," I whisper, my voice gone from shaky to nonexistent.

DR. ASHA had explained that some treatments have shown a side effect of producing strange or vivid dreams, but that isn't expected with the pills I'm taking now. So that doesn't explain what happened that night.

I woke up beside Nick.

There he was, snoring softly with his bare back to me. I reached out to touch him, to see if he was real. He stirred, woke, and turned over. With a contented smile on his lips, he murmured, "Hi, baby."

"Nick...?"

"I know. I missed you too. Of course I came back."

He reached up to stroke my face and started kissing me. Next thing I knew, he was straddling me and I felt safer than ever. I always felt protected with him. I wanted to feel like that again, I wanted to be with him and make love again, right that moment.

And then he stopped, moved away from me, got out of bed.

"Sorry. I've got to go," was all he said, fully dressed again. And he walked out of the room.

There's a heavy sadness in my chest telling me I'm awake, for real this time. A queasy chill washes over me, and I can't tell whether it's because of the pills or because I miss Nick so much.

It's still dark outside, and it's started raining. I don't want to ring Freddie and Marcus; they'd likely want to run over and keep me company. I've got to get through this on my own, at least the first time. Anyway, Marcus said he'd give me a call in the morning and remind me about taking the next dose.

That's the last fucking thing I want to be reminded of at the moment.

CHAPTER 18

THOSE first few days after starting treatment... you really don't want to know. Of everything I've been through since coming back from Ibiza, I'd say that was the worst, except for actually finding another man beside Nick. I have never felt so sick—not after all-night piss-ups, not after the dodgiest curries, not even when I was in hospital with pneumonia.

The hardest part, besides feeling physically ill all day, is how defeated I feel. I'd wondered if I was making an awful mistake when I took that first dose, and now I'm sure I have. I felt okay before starting treatment, maybe I wasn't feeling 100 percent back to normal yet, but I was doing pretty well. Now I've voluntarily taken medication which is making me feel awful, and try as I might, I cannot see the sense of it.

I know, I know... the side effects will more than likely go away soon, I can manage them until they do, and I need to take medications to stop the disease progressing. You know what? Fuck that. I did *not* feel sick before. I sure as hell do now. What kind of game is this supposed to be? "Oh, sorry you've got HIV, mate. Take these and it'll stop you dying straight away. Oh, but they might make you *wish* you were dead."

I guess I'm not very good company at the moment. That's why I'm surprised that Krist has taken it upon himself to keep me company these last few days. Given what he said about refusing to take meds after his first treatment made him sick, I figured he would be the last person to want to hang out with me while I'm feeling like this. But when he came by Tuesday morning because he didn't see me at breakfast, I told him I'd taken my second dose of treatment that morning and was feeling like death warmed up, he sat right down beside me.

I wasn't wrong when I reckoned him for a good distraction. When he saw how really miserable I was, he brought round his DVD sets of *The Royle Family* and *Queer as Folk* to keep me entertained and, as he put it, to remind me how much worse my life could be—and *would* be if I ever dared travel north of London. Krist made it his personal mission to stay with me as much as possible these days. Between him hanging out, Marcus ringing a couple times a day, and Freddie compulsively texting me, I'm glad I've got mates who care.

I REALLY considered not going to the group meeting Thursday evening. I'm not feeling quite as horrendous as I was, though, and I really do want to be there. I figure I can always duck out early if I really need to.

Freddie is with Marcus at the meeting this week. He tells me they attend together as much as possible. It's kind of amazing how much more mature Freddie is these days. Before, I would never have figured him for spending one evening a week at a support group with his partner. Of course, I also didn't think last week at my first meeting that I'd ever see my best mate here.

There's another bloke who wasn't here last week as well. He looks to be just a little younger than me, and he's sitting off to the end of the semicircle, looking nervous. I know I felt the same way last week, and I'm just about to go over and introduce myself when Jarrod moves to the front of the circle. I guess there will be plenty of introductions in a minute anyway.

"All right, lads. We've got another new attendee with us tonight," Jarrod says. "I'd like you all to meet Trevor."

There's a general round of "heys" and "hellos," to which Trevor nods but doesn't really meet anyone's eyes. He doesn't say anything in response either.

Instead of going around and everyone giving their introductions, Jarrod moves us on to other topics. I get the sense that he's taking it easy on Trevor, who looks like he could do with the thoughtfulness just now. Jarrod asks if anyone has any news or anything they'd like to share. Jarrod had been round to see me Tuesday afternoon, and we'd talked about a few things—settling in, starting treatment... and finding my best mate again.

Glancing over, Freddie and I nod at one another.

"You all remember when I first starting coming here with Marc, I'd recently fallen out with a good mate. Turns out, he's back with us." Freddie reaches out and squeezes my shoulder.

For a moment most of the group looks a bit gobsmacked, unsurprisingly, but then offer congrats. I also mention that I've started treatment and it's going kind of rough at the moment, but that I am doing my best to cope with it. Again, most everyone offers their support any time I need it. It makes me realize just how much it means to me to have friends here, and how incredible it really is that I've again found my best mate, here as well.

A couple other guys have some general news. Martin is thinking of donating a memorial garden in the park to Gier. Beside me, Krist leans over, kisses my cheek, and says, "I have just spent these last days keeping Pad-babe in good spirits. Thankfully, he will *not* have to return the favor." Okay, so he's a twat, but a lovable one.

I've noticed Mick has been quiet and withdrawn the whole time, more than he was at that yoga session on Monday. When it comes to his turn to share news, he hunches forward, leaning his elbows on his knees, and is quiet for a few moments. When he finally talks, his voice sounds gravelly and low. "Oisin's sick," he says.

Marcus reaches over to squeeze his hand with a mien that says he knows the feeling all too well.

"I'm so scared," Mick whispers thickly, covering his face with his other hand. "He's slipping away from me, and I can't do anything about it."

"It's the hardest thing in the world," Marcus says softly.

"We're here, Mick," Martin says.

"Even if all we can do to help is listen," Allen adds.

"I don't want to be without him," Mick says, and it sounds like he's swallowed rusty nails. "He's my entire world. I'm terrified when I think of never seeing him again."

There's a shaky sob at the end of the circle from the new bloke. Trevor breaks down in tears and tries to wipe them away with trembling hands. "I just want him back," he chokes out. "I don't give a fuck about anything else, I just want him back again!"

Jarrod moves to wrap an arm around Trevor's shoulders, but Trevor gets up and crosses to the door, saying, "I can't, I'm sorry. I can't just now."

"Poor babe," Krist murmurs.

"He's going through hell on earth," Martin says, to which Marcus nods.

"Trevor needs a lot of support," Jarrod says quietly. "We'll need to be gentle about it. Just earlier today he said he felt like he was ready to at least sit in with us. You guys know how it goes, though. For some people, some days are better than others. For others, some *minutes* are better than others."

THE next morning on my way downstairs to grab some brekkie, two other people step into the hallway at the same time. One I don't recognize, leaving Krist's flat and looking rough. The other is Trevor from last night. I pick up the pace to catch him up.

"Hey, good morning," I say with a wave, hoping to make him feel at least a little better than he did last night.

Trevor stops and seems surprised that I'm talking to him. "Oh. Hi. Um...."

"I'm Padrig," I offer my hand and he accepts it with a little hesitation. "I'm new here as well, only been a week now."

"Nice to meet you. I'm Trevor, but Jarrod mentioned that already. I'm... I'm really sorry about last night. You all probably think I'm a complete head case."

"Nah, it's not like that here," I assure him. "You don't have to apologize or explain. I think everybody understands that sometimes it's just too hard."

"Thanks. It's not like that all the time, but the last couple weeks have been hard for me."

I nod in understanding. "I was just heading down to get some grub. Do you want to grab a bite?"

"Okay, yeah," he says.

Over breakfast, Trevor talks to me about his partner, Finley. "I just don't know what to do without him," he says. "That's why I decided to come here. I just don't want to be alone. Of course, half the time all I want is to be left alone." He shrugs. "I know I need to get myself together again though. Fin would hate seeing me like this."

"Maybe he'd understand that it takes some time," I tell him, even though I didn't know his partner. "It's really hard losing someone you love."

"He was totally patient," Trevor says, and then goes quiet for a bit. "You know what the hardest thing is though?"

I shake my head.

"He wasn't even sick. He was healthier than a lot of negative people. If it had been the virus that finally took him, at least that I could have understood. That was what we expected, you know. I couldn't even bear to go to his funeral. Haven't been to the grave either. He wanted to be cremated, but his family wouldn't have it."

"What happened?" I ask, then add quickly, "I mean, if you want to talk about it. You don't have to."

Trevor shakes his head. "It was an accident. On the M11, near A120."

"I'm sorry."

"Thanks."

"I know it doesn't help much to hear that."

"It does, though, to have people care even a little bit right now."

"Yeah, I know that as well. Talking makes things easier, I've found, but being around good people means the most when you're having a bad time."

"I definitely feel a little better this morning. I owe you one, Padrig."

I smile and tell him I'll keep that in mind.

THAT evening I'm feeling well enough to have a go at making my own dinner, the first time I've cooked in my new place. Krist decides to join me, saying that I shouldn't eat alone, but he brings his own dinner. I'm doing rice with a coconut sauce and some veggies. Krist's takeaway looks like some kind of chop suey loaded with MSG. Krist teases me that I "even eat like a queer," but that doesn't stop him nobbling a bit of mine as we're sat in front of the telly watching *Corrie*.

I try not to remember those Friday night takeaways with Nick. The way he used to wrap an arm around my shoulders and lean in to kiss my jawline, while reaching into my stir-fry to pluck out those little miniature corn bits. I don't particularly like them anyway and would just give them to him, but Nick liked to think he's distracting me with romance. I always told him he could have the corn, as long as he left my nuts alone. He never agreed to that and told me *my* nuts are the best and how unfair it would be to deprive him of them.

Krist offers to do the washing up as repayment for letting him taste some of my dinner. I did say he's a loveable twat, right? When he sits back down with me, he hands me a cup of plump berries for dessert. He says that he was going to bring a big chocolate cake, but he's trying to mind his figure. And mine. I shove at his shoulder and call him a wanker, but he is quick to correct me. He tells me, quite proudly, that he has not gotten himself off in over five years. I'm about to say that I find that claim dubious at best, but I consider that it is Krist I'm talking to and one shouldn't apply conventional expectations to him.

"I have a feeling that's probably the only way I'll ever get off again," I mumble.

"Ah now, Pad-babe. There are plenty of fish in the sea," Krist says, wrapping his arm around me.

"Yeah right, *too* many. I just want love again."

"Not me," Krist says. "I don't fear dying, but I could not be in a relationship. I think it would make it harder to die. If I had love, the real sort, I would want to stay with him and not hurt him. At least this way, everything is up to me."

"I guess I can see what you mean about not wanting to put someone through that loss." Just having seen how affected Marcus, Mick, and Trevor have been by their partners' suffering, I can tell how difficult it is for someone to lose their significant other like that. But.... "I think it would be easier, though, knowing there's someone there for you, who maybe you can hope to find again in the next life, whatever that may be."

Krist just smiles at me, kisses my cheek, and tucks my head against his shoulder. Before long, I find myself dozing off beside him.

CHAPTER 19

SATURDAY afternoon, Trevor and I decided to have a go at the fitness room. I always used to spend a few hours a week in the gym; even when I had to force myself to go, I was always glad I had done by the time I left. Dr. Asha recommended that it could help with getting adjusted to the meds, as well as being good for me in general. I'm glad Trevor came along so we keep one another from overdoing it.

Nevertheless, we're both worn out by the time we head back up to my kitchenette for some lunch. It's a relief enough to actually *want* to have lunch after the way I've felt since Tuesday. I'm still not feeling entirely brilliant, but it's gotten a lot better already. A lot of the credit goes to Marc for his eating suggestions, like having a cup of ginger or mint tea a few times a day, leaving off anything citrus, and some creative variations of the BRAT diet that have kept me from getting tired of applesauce and rice.

"Are we pathetic or something?" Trevor asks, sprawling out on my couch. "I thought I was fit. I mean, haven't been to the gym since before Christmas, but I thought I was doing alright."

"We might well be pathetic," I agree, shoving in beside him. "I used to keep fit, but I guess I lost a lot of it."

Trevor looks over at me, with some effort to roll his head in my direction. "Is it okay if I ask what happened? If you don't want to talk about it, I understand."

"It's okay. Kind of a long story, though. Basically, I came home to find my boyfriend in bed with someone else. I guess I kind of did a runner and ended up crying in the park until this guy came along and offered me the 'tea and sympathy' line. What I didn't know was that he'd drugged the tea and planned to keep me like that for a while."

"Oh shit," Trevor murmurs, then pulls me into a hug.

As much as I appreciate his concern, it's becoming a bit repetitive, this reaction whenever I tell someone what happened. It's surprising that it seems to be getting easier to talk about, though. That seems like it could be a good thing, that I'm moving past it. But it also seems like it's too soon and I've missed some steps along the way. Jarrod has said to me a few times, though, that there is no "right" way to experience the grieving process and that the steps might shift around a bit. So I figure it's probably best not to worry about it. As long as I am taking the time to talk to him about it during our sessions, I think it'll be okay.

Anyway, I've promised Marc to go along with him to the theatre tonight, so I don't want to be in a down mood. Freddie is playing Dogberry in a small local troupe's production of *Much Ado About Nothing*. When we were in school we used to go out for as many school plays as we could. Freddie decided to keep with it as a hobby.

The last time I saw Freddie on stage was when I'd first started dating Nick. It was *The Importance of Being Earnest*, and I mostly remember that night as being the first time Nick and I slept together. I tell myself to just stop reacting the way I do every time I think of him, but I know it's not as easy as that. How do you stop that clenching sensation in your gut and the pang in your heart when you fear that you've forever lost your chance to have real love in your life?

SUNDAY night, Krist and I are stretched out on my couch watching telly. He's brought round his *Queer as Folk* DVDs again. Krist is saying something about how Stuart was his top idol until he turned pussy for Vince, who was too much of a pussy to be "properly" gay, and Nathan was just too… Nathan.

I really have no clue what he's on about; all I can think at the moment is one thing. I slide a little closer to Krist and reach up to touch his cheek. He cocks his head at me, and I gaze back for a moment or two before closing the distance and pressing our lips together. It's not enough, and I shove my tongue into his mouth, searching for the feeling I'm missing. It's been so long since I've kissed someone who I *wanted* to kiss. I get a little overeager as I push Krist back and practically climb on top of him.

It takes me a moment to register that Krist isn't really kissing me back and is gently pushing at my shoulder. I scramble back to the other end of the couch, out of breath and horridly embarrassed.

Krist pulls me back beside him and hugs me tightly. "Pad-babe, I'm fucking flattered, but this is not what you need, love."

"What I need? How the fuck do you know what I need?" I whisper, refusing to look at him. "It obviously works for you."

"Padrig, we have experienced similar situations, but that does not mean we have the same solutions. We are different, babe. I love you, but not the way you are looking for."

Unexpected tears of frustration rush up and slip from my eyes. Shouting, I shove Krist away as I jump up from the couch, pacing and clenching my fists.

"What kind of hope do I have?" I ask him loudly. "Who the fuck would even think of loving someone like me? Look at me! I was fucked up in the first place, I couldn't stand to go down on my boyfriends because of what that prick in school did, and now I've spent ten months of my life being drugged and whored—and I'm going to die because of it! I don't know if I'll ever be able to let a man fuck me again anyway, and all I want is to be loved again, but who the hell is going to love someone they never even get to shag? Of everything those fuckers took from me, why did they have to take the one thing that was the most important to me!"

That's followed by a proper breakdown, me sliding down to the floor and lying against the couch, sobbing and hiccoughing. Krist doesn't say anything; he just sits down beside me and pulls me into his arms again, rocking me slowly and letting me cry on his shoulder.

It's a while before I calm down a little, and by then I'm pretty exhausted. Still holding Krist like an anchor in a tempest, I murmur an apology for "all of that." He just runs a hand over my hair and shushes me.

"Will you stay with me?" I ask him, sounding like I've swallowed sand.

"Of course I will. Now, you should be in bed, Pad-babe. Come on," Krist says softly.

Krist stands me up with him and walks me into the bedroom. He helps me out of my clothes down to my boxers and tucks me into bed before lying down beside me, on top of the quilt. He cuddles up beside me and wraps an arm around me. I'm asleep almost immediately, but not before I hear Krist whisper, "*Schlaf, mein Süßer*. I would love you like that if I could."

WHEN I wake up Monday morning there's no one in my bed but me, and I'm a little disappointed. I'd kind of hoped Krist might stay with me, but I realize I probably scared him with my little rant, and pushing myself on him like that. I don't feel like lying here analyzing that breakdown any further, so I get up and shrug into a dressing gown, intent on fixing a cup of tea as quickly as possible.

Wandering into the kitchenette, I have to wonder just how a mixing bowl full of flour got itself there. I wasn't cooking last night, and I'm sure I'd have done the washing up better than that anyway.

My front door bangs closed, and Krist walks in with a couple of eggs in one hand. "Had to run down to mine," he says, kissing my cheek. "Sit and relax, I am doing breakfast for us. Tea is brewing in the pot on the table, should be ready to pour."

"Thanks, mate," I say, pulling him into a hug and hoping he understands how much it means to me that he didn't leave in the night.

Krist pats my head with his free hand and turns back to the mixing bowl. "So, what was it that prick from school did to you?" he asks, as if we're discussing the weather forecast.

For a moment I'm not sure what he's talking about, then I remember that I probably blurted that out last night. "Ancient history, Krist," I mumble.

"Repressing things is not healthy for you," he says seriously, looking back at me over his shoulder.

"I didn't repress it. Nick knew."

"Well, Krist does not. And Krist wants to know so that he can beat the shit out of the bastard who hurt his sweet Pad-babe."

I can't help grinning at Krist. "Good luck with that one, mate. I heard that arsehole bit it in a bike crash a few years ago. Brains all over the roadway."

"What brains?" Krist scoffs. "Too fucking good for him. I wanted to do him over properly," he pouts. "Ah well. What did happen, babe?"

With a sigh, I take a long sip of tea. The heat of the mug cradled in my hands is soothing. "Okay. I was like sixteen, and he was my first serious crush. Not just like ones when you're thirteen and fancy your maths teacher or the boy who sits in front of you in English literature. I knew he was gay because one time I'd seen him making out with his wrestling partner in the lockers, but I knew they weren't a 'couple' either. I got up the nerve to tell him that I fancied him, and he called me a pathetic faggot and walked away. I was pretty well down about it until a few days later when he came up to me in the gents and asked if I was still interested. I said I was, and he said he'd let me suck his cock right then. I had no idea what I was doing, but I agreed because I wanted him so much. He just shoved his dick in my mouth and fucked my face, didn't even warn me when he was coming. There I was, sat there on the floor, gagging with my eyes all watery, and he just did up his trousers and left me like that. Well, I thought that was how oral sex always went and I hated it so much I refused to do it again."

Krist sets a plate of crepes and berries in front of me and sits down with me. "The arse was probably just intimidated because you are so beautiful. I am not sure that any man could control himself in that pretty mouth of yours," he winks. A dubious compliment coming from anyone else, but Krist means it well.

Neither of us say much for a while, which ought to tell you how good Krist's cooking is. I could really bulk up if I keep him around. After a while, Krist reaches for the teapot to refill his mug, then looks up at me and says, "I think you should try to find him, babe."

"I told you, that guy carked it years ago." I've no idea why he's so fixated on something I got over ages ago.

"Not the arsehole. I mean your Nick."

Taking a deep breath, I shake my head. "I couldn't do that."

"I think you need it," Krist says. "You are not over him, and I think you have unresolved issues with him to be addressed."

"Krist, I... I can't. He's gone back to the States, for one thing, and I rather doubt I can pop off there at the moment."

"Geoff is your advocate, yes?"

"Yeah, but... I mean, flying to the States to look for an ex-boyfriend?"

Krist grins. "You would be surprised. He gets all manner of things set up. Anyway, I just think you should think about it, babe."

"I don't know, Krist. I guess I could ask him about it."

"Just do, babe. Never know what could come of it."

Maybe he's right. Maybe I do need closure.

CHAPTER 20

THE next week is a bit busy for me. I think I'm getting to have a regular schedule, though. Yoga is Monday, Tuesday's my appointments with Jarrod, Wednesday I have lunch with Geoff, and Thursday is the group meeting. Of course, none of these things take a great deal of time in my day, but it is good to have things to do, to have a sort of structure.

Tuesday, I talked to Jarrod about what happened Sunday night, and about maybe trying to find Nick again. I think he sort of agreed with Krist that my reaction probably had a lot to do with missing Nick and the fact that I really had no closure with him. A part of me wants to say it's better to try to let it go and not open old wounds, but then again, those wounds aren't so old, and they're definitely not healed well.

So during our lunch appointment on Wednesday, I decided to ask Geoff whether it would be possible. Geoff leans back in his chair with his iced latte and says, "Well, Padrig, financially speaking it would certainly be feasible. I've said before, you have no worries about that. However, I don't think there's much I can do about the legal aspects, at least not in the short term."

"My passport is still in date." I'd had it renewed just before the Ibiza trip.

"Yes it is, but… well, afraid it wouldn't do you any good for entering the United States. You see, there are travel restrictions for HIV-positive travelers," Geoff says gently.

"Are you serious?" I ask, glad I didn't just take a drink of tea punch.

"I am. You could possibly apply for a special waiver, but those are not at all easy to get and tricky to maintain."

"Do you mean that... I couldn't leave the country?" I ask quietly.

"Oh, by all means you can. There are many places that have no such restrictions. Unfortunately, the US does. I would be more than happy to help you find contact information for Nick, though."

I thank him and tell him I'll let him know if a time comes when I'm ready for that. At the moment I'm feeling quite deflated. I can't understand; it's not like I'm a danger to people just being in their country. And last time I checked, the US wasn't exactly insulated against HIV. I guess I'm beginning to realize the amount of discrimination that I may have to deal with because of my health status. As if being gay weren't enough in the first place.

AT THE Thursday meeting, I have to admit that I'm feeling a bit down from learning about the travel restrictions. Most of the group can sympathize with the saddening and frustrating feeling of pointless sero-discrimination.

Martin says that his partner Gier was let go from his job as an industrial engineer after his superiors found out he was positive. "We considered filing a suit against his company," he says, "but we decided that we didn't want to spend our time together dealing with ugly things like courts. I might do it now he's gone, though, for others like him."

Christian says that he and Clyde were asked to leave their development after someone found out about Clyde. As he put it, "it was alright when we were just the queers on the street, but they fucking shit themselves when somebody said HIV was in the neighborhood." Christian's language drew a raised brow from Clyde, and Christian quickly apologized with a little kiss to Clyde's cheek.

"It was family for me," Allen says. "My father stopped speaking to me when I came out; mum didn't until I told her about my test result. She said I'd good as committed suicide. That's when I decided to come here and found *real* family." He tries to call up one of his warm smiles, but it's more wan than usual and I hope he's doing okay.

If nothing else, it's at least comforting to know that I'm not the only one who's felt discriminated against. Not that I'd ever want others to experience this. It does help, though, letting others hear what you've been through and finding out that you aren't alone. By the time the meeting is adjourned I'm feeling better and decide to invite a few of the guys up to mine for afters.

Freddie and Marc, Krist, and Trevor come up to have a taste of the crepes I made with Krist's recipe. I got some fresh mango from down in the kitchen shop this morning to go with them. As I'm making up plates and passing them round, I mention not seeing Mick at the meeting or at yoga on Monday. Krist says that Oisin has been in hospital for the last few days and Mick won't leave him any longer than it takes to go down to the café and bring something back up to the room. I can't help thinking that doesn't sound good at all.

"Well hey," Freddie says after a quiet moment, "you guys ought to come down to Form with us next Friday. We're having a welcome-home party for Archie."

"Archie's back? When?" Freddie mentioned that he was abroad on a work trip, and I've been hoping to see him again when he returned.

"Getting back tonight. You ought to come round for dinner tomorrow, we'll surprise him," Freddie grins. "He'll be floored!"

"You guys hang out at Form?" Trevor asks like he's not sure what to think.

"Oh yeah, we used to spend just about every weekend there, Pad and Arch and I. People used to think we owned the place, we were there so often. We kind of quit going after you went missing, Pad, but I think it would be brilliant for us all to go again. Good times, that."

"Is it really a sex club?" Trevor asks.

Freddie and I exchange looks and a laugh. "Not unless you count dry humping on the dance floor," Freddie says. "Well, things do go on in the gents, but I'm not at liberty to speak about those things...."

"Oh. Finley and I were always kind of interested in going, but we'd heard some things that turned us off about it," Trevor says. "I think I'd trust you lot, though."

"Brilliant! We'll plan on it, then. You in as well, Krist?"

Krist smirks. "I will be there before you. You will see me, I am... flamboyant. Unless I find a good reason to leave early."

FREDDIE stops round after work the next day to give me a lift over to their place. As soon as we get there, Marcus asks me I would mind coming with him to pick up a few things for the dinner he's doing up. I get the feeling that something is a little off with him, but I'm not sure what. Freddie said Archie would be round in a bit, and I don't mind having a walk to let off some nervous energy anyway.

"Sorry I'm dragging you out again first thing," Marcus says as we're walking down their street. "I'm a little pissed at Fred and just wanted to vent."

"What you mad about?" Freddie seemed fine on the ride over, so I'm guessing the argument is mostly one-way.

"Last night when we got home, he mentioned that he doesn't care much for the idea of you trying to get in touch with your old boyfriend again. I know he's trying to look out for you, that's a good thing and all, but I told him he needs to mind his own business and let you make your own choices. And that's what I'm telling you, too, Padrig. If you feel like you need to see him or talk to him again...." Marcus stops and takes a breath. "I'm just saying, Pad, only you know what you need to do. And if you need help finding a way to do it, we'll help you. I sure as hell will, anyway."

"Thanks, Marc. I appreciate that," I tell him, giving him a shoulder hug. "I'm not surprised Freddie's got his opinion on that. He's always been like that, I don't blame him or anything. Honestly, though, I don't know if it would be any use at the moment. Geoff offered me help contacting him as well, but... I don't know. The conversation I'd need to have with him isn't one I really want to do over the phone. Maybe at some point, if I know I just need to clear things with him, I'll let you lot know. For right now, I think I need to work on *me* for a while first."

"Okay," Marcus nods. "As long as you're in touch with what you need. I'm sorry for getting all worked up over that, but something similar almost happened to me and Jamey. I kind of accused him of cheating on me and we were officially not together for a few months. He gave in and called me when he started having signs of PML and was told he probably didn't have much longer. I had one friend at the time who told me again and again that I should just forget his cheating ass, but I knew I couldn't."

"What happened?" I ask quietly.

"He wasn't cheating. The person I'd seen him out with, and talking quietly on the phone with, was his solicitor and they were working on his will. He didn't want to talk to me about it because he was afraid it would upset me, silly bastard. Even if he had been seeing someone else, I never regretted listening to my heart instead of a 'voice of reason', just that one time. What we had was worth more than that. That was when we went up to Scotland and got 'married'. That's the photo I showed you in the dining room. If I'd missed those last months with him, difficult as they were, I'd have never forgiven myself. Anyway, I know the situation was different with your boyfriend, but... I just mean, Pad, you have to trust yourself on this. Advice is a great thing, but sometimes you're going to hear a lot of conflicting advice, and that's when you need to go with your gut."

"Thanks, Marc. What did you need for dinner down here anyway?" We've been walking down South Leigh for a while and passed a couple little markets already.

Marc shakes his head. "Nothing. I just needed to get that off my chest. So you don't think I should be too pissed off at Fred on your behalf?"

"Nah. I can handle him and his opinions. Been doing since we were at school."

"Thank fuck. I was really hoping to get some later tonight!"

"Bloody hell. I didn't need to know that!"

Marcus just snickers and turns back toward their place. He does at least pop into one market to pick up a few pieces of fruit, to justify dashing out. As soon as we get up to their flat, Marc shoves his shopping onto the kitchen worktop and wraps his arms around Freddie, who's mixing a couple of drinks. Clearly Marc knows how to drop an argument, and their quick kiss gives me a sort of wistful, bittersweet smile as I watch from the doorway between the kitchen and entryway.

I've known Freddie a long time, and I know he's always wanted someone to love and care for. Most of the time, though, he was the one in our group without a date. He's far from being a troll or shy or anything. I always thought he was just too romantic, deep down. One-nighters always left him feeling more down than smug. I'm glad he found such a stable thing with Marc.

Freddie glances over and winks at me. "Oi, Jock! Why don't ya get off yer lazy arse and come fetch your own drink!" he shouts into the lounge.

"And you wonder why I like being abroad for weeks and missing that sort of abuse!"

I know it's Archie as soon as I hear that Glaswegian accent call back. He comes around the corner from the lounge, looking like he's ready to give Freddie a stinging comeback, but he stops when he sees me. He sort of does a double take, his bright eyes going wide.

"Oh my god," he murmurs after a shocked moment. "Padrig?"

"Hey, mate," I say, almost as if I'd seen him just before he left on his business trip.

"Padrig!" Archie repeats in a shriller tone. "I'm seein' things!"

I shrug and shake my head.

"Bloody hell…," he says under his breath. He breaks out of the "trance" he was in and in two steps is wrapping me up in a suffocating hug. "I missed you so much, Pad! God, look at you!" he says, taking a step back again and looking me over. "Cut your hair, and you're skinnier than you were. When did you come round again? I've been away for a few weeks, but Freddie didn' say owt that you were back again! Where've you been, what've you been doing all this time?"

Archie's prattling was always particularly endearing. I could just listen to him babble on excitedly in that sometimes unintelligible brogue of his.

"It's a pretty long story, mate. Maybe we ought to have a sit?"

"Yeah, yeah. Freddie was just making a couple gin and tonics. Want one?" he asks, absently taking the drink Freddie hands him from the kitchen and pulling me toward the lounge.

"No, I'm okay, thanks." I figure he'll need the drink by the time I'm done with my story though. Archie is one person to whom I almost hate to talk about this. He was always quite empathetic, and I do hope he doesn't take my situation too hard.

Sitting together on Marc and Freddie's couch, I'm surprised that Archie doesn't go teary-eyed or pull me into a big hug like most people do after hearing about my ordeal and diagnosis. He just reaches for my hand and says I'm the bravest person he's ever met and how dead proud he is of me for fighting and taking my life back. He's really wonderfully supportive, and I don't feel at all guilty for breaking bad news to him. It's not that I blame anyone else for their reactions, I never would, but it is kind of a relief to have someone *respond* to what I tell them, instead of *reacting*.

The four of us spend the entire evening hanging out at Freddie and Marc's. It's so much like how things used to be that I almost forget I'll be going back to my own flat... alone. I try to tell myself that I am not alone, I've got a lot of really wonderful friends, new and old, who love me and support me.

CHAPTER
21

MONDAY morning next, I've got another appointment with Dr. Asha. It's a fortnight now since I started treatment. I have to admit I do feel better; the side effects aren't bothering me nearly as much. This appointment is so Dr. Asha can run tests to find out if the meds are working yet. Marc's come with me again, and he's a good friend for holding my hand without laughing about it when Dr. Asha draws a blood sample from me.

She says she'll ring me with the results and that we'll be hoping for a reduction of my "viral load" and an increase in my CD4 count. According to Dr. Asha, I'm doing really well with everything else as far as she can tell. She's pleased that I'm serious about taking my medication properly, despite having a tough time with it at first, and that I'm eating well, taking up yoga, and gradually working into a gym routine. Most of all, though, I think she's really happy that I've got such supportive mates, new and old. I have to admit that I'm quite chuffed with myself as well.

THE week goes well, if a bit slow. I'm mostly waiting for Friday night to go to Form with the lads. It'll be the first time I've been out to party with mates in a very long time. I sure as hell don't count those trips to the club with Alex.

I'm especially glad that Trevor agreed to come along with us. I think he could do with a night out with mates; he's been opening up more and spending time with Krist and me quite a bit. A part of me wonders if he is ready for going out to a place like Form, but he's a grown man, can make up his own mind, and if he wants to be off we'll make sure he gets back here.

After dinner at Marc and Freddie's, the five of us—Trevor, Archie, Marc, Freddie, and I—squeeze into Freddie's bright orange Focus. It's only a fifteen-minute ride to the club and a few minutes' walk on a nice evening. We're early enough that the wait is only a few minutes as well. There were times when we used to come here it would take half an hour to get in.

We find ourselves a table overlooking the dance floor, and Archie offers to pick up the first round. Marc and I opt for ginger ale, while Trevor goes for a low-alcohol lager. Archie and Freddie, naturally, go for Long Islands.

There's a weird déjà vu feeling as I stand at the table, looking over the crowd that's undulating to the deep bass. I've been to this place more times than I can count, so it would make sense to remember it clearly, but this is different. It's more like I *can't* remember it clearly, like it's all a bit fuzzy and the details are lost. I try to shrug it off—it has been a while since I've been here—and just enjoy the evening with my mates.

Krist waves and blows a kiss from down on the dance floor where there's at least three guys being very obvious about vying for his attention. I'm not remotely surprised, especially given the skin-tight, sheer shirt he's got on. Archie's gone off to chat someone up, and Marc's pulled Freddie onto the floor. I'm not really keen on dancing or flirting, so I stick by Trevor, letting people think we're a couple. We can just hang out and enjoy the show. Trevor seems to be enjoying himself, smiling more than I've ever seen him and having a laugh at the trolls who think they're going to pull with twinks whose IDs are queerer than they are. Having such a good time with mates in one of my old favorite places is enough for me to get over that weird sensation and feel like this is a homecoming for me as well as Archie.

At one point later in the evening, I notice Krist waving at us again, this time as he's leaving the club with a hot catch. I'm guessing he's only stayed as long as he has because we're here as well. Deciding it's a good time for a slash, I go down the stairs and cross the club in the direction I know the back toilets to be. I'm hoping it's still early enough that there won't be much (or any) spillover from the ones near the front of the club. It's a bit difficult to have a piss while everyone around you is having some kind of hurry-up sex.

Going toward to the back, I notice a dark, heavy curtain that someone's put up over a doorway. I'm struck with a tense and lightheaded feeling, like someone has taken hold and given me a rough shaking. How many times have I been here with my mates, with Nick, and assumed that was a utility cupboard they wanted to mask over? Now that déjà vu feeling makes sense, I know what was behind that curtain, not very long ago. Me.

I feel sick, and it's not the meds. I only just make it to the men's room, drug-hazed memories coming back to me in a rush, memories I'd hoped to forget forever. Falling to my knees, I retch with hot tears running down my face. This place was practically a home-away-from-home for us… how could it have also been a place of so much misery?

I hear someone else enter the loo, but I ignore it. Whoever they are will have seen men sick in clubs, I'm sure. I feel a hand on my shoulder and figure it's one of the lads come to find me. I'm about to say I'll be all right, until I hear the man speak.

"Too much to drink?" he asks in a thick Russian accent. "Happens all the time."

He steps away before I can respond, and I hear him running taps. That man who took me out of here, he had the same accent, as well as a "Glasgow smile" on the right side of his face. I'm afraid to look back and see that scar. Moments later he returns and puts a cool, wet cloth on the back of my neck.

"Come, sit back, is more comfortable," he says, his hand on my shoulder, encouraging me to lean back against the wall.

"It's you, isn't it?" I rasp, keeping my eyes shut.

"If you mean we have met before, yes."

He continues to hold the cloth against my neck, and I finally risk a glance at him, seeing the scar I knew was there. I'm unable to stop myself asking, "Who are you? Why did you help me?"

"You reminded me of Petya," he says quietly. The way he looks at me conveys a deep loss, whoever Petya was. Then he seems to come back to himself and continues. "You see, I am a businessman and have recently acquired this nightclub. I own several other establishments, and I do not like to see my customers unhappy with the service. Some of the things going on here when I came, they were... bad for business. Those things had to be... removed. I run a clean establishment."

The man takes the cloth from the back of my neck, shakes it out, and folds it neatly before putting it into the pocket of his sharp black suit. "You should be alright now. You do not have to worry about seeing anything bad here ever again. I make certain of that personally. Glad you are doing well, Padrig. Stay well." He stands and walks out of the gents before I can say anything else.

A few moments of incredulity pass before I attempt to push myself up from the floor of the loo and wash my mouth out in the sink. Just then Archie comes in.

"You alright, lad?" he asks, ducking into one of the stalls.

Thinking about it for a moment, I respond, "Yeah. I'm okay, Arch. Just... surprised by something I saw." I splash a little water on my face to wash away the tear tracks. "I think I've probably had enough of a night for just now, though."

"I was just coming to tell you we're talking of heading off," Archie says, flushing and coming out to wash his hands. "You sure you're okay?" he asks, cocking his head curiously.

"I am. I'm with my mates, everything is fine." I put my arm around Archie's shoulder as we're about to go back out into the club.

"Actually, I wanted to ask you about something," he says, pulling me back a bit. "Your mate, Trevor?"

"Yeah?"

"Anything there?" Archie shrugs a shoulder.

I hesitate, realizing Archie is asking what *I* think of Trevor. "I don't really think I'm ready to be thinking about that kind of thing yet. Actually, I'm pretty sure Trev isn't either. He only lost his boyfriend recently and it was really rough for him."

"I know, I'm not saying you should rush anything. I'm just thinking of down the road, you know? At some point, in the right time. You deserve someone good."

He always gives me a smile, Archie. "Thanks, Arch. You're a good bloke. I don't care what anybody says."

Archie claps my shoulder and follows me out of the gents before stopping and frowning. "Oi. What's *that* supposed to mean?!" he cries, half drowned out by the music, hurrying after me back to our table.

CHAPTER 22

I'M UP a little late on Saturday morning; guess I needed some extra sleep after being out. That was never the case with me before. I used to be up by 8:00 a.m. no matter how late I was out. Nick was the one who could sleep past noon. At least I'm not late for taking my meds, though Marc has been ringing me at 8:50 every morning and evening to remind me.

I think this morning I'd rather go downstairs for fresh-made food than be bothered doing anything up. Once again, there's someone going out from Krist's flat just as I'm stepping into the hallway, only this time Krist follows him out.

"See you round," his date says quietly, looking like he's expecting a kiss.

"*Das ist fraglich*," Krist says with a grin. "Sorry, that is German for 'of course'. *Wiedersehen*!"

Krist walks toward me and into my flat, leaving the other guy to find his own way out.

Krist drapes himself over half of my couch as I ask, "Why do I get the feeling 'fraglich' is *not* 'of course'?"

"Close enough," he says. "Come sit?"

"I'm really not up for juicy details just yet," I protest. Not that I don't go ahead and sit by Krist anyway. "Haven't even had brekkie."

"We shall go in a moment. I wanted to give you the news first, though."

SINS OF ANOTHER

"What news?" I ask with a frown. I don't think Krist is about to announce he's marrying that one-nighter.

"Jarrod rang me this morning. It was about Oisin, Mick's partner."

Can't be good news. "Is he...."

Krist nods with a sigh. "Sometime last night."

I didn't know Oisin, but it's still sad to hear. Anyone could see that Mick loved him with everything he had; it was plain just in the few times I was around him. I really can't imagine how difficult this must be for Mick.

I'VE no idea how it's been managed—either Mick or Oisin's family must know some rather influential individuals—because Sunday afternoon a lot of us from the Thursday night group go to the funeral home together. I had thought Krist heard wrong, it was meant to be the Sunday next—that's how long it usually takes—but Jarrod confirmed that the visitation is in fact this same weekend.

I ride along with Freddie, Marc, Krist, and Allen, while Martin, Christian, and Clyde go with Jarrod. It's slow going to get through the crowds of visitors. I get the feeling that a lot of these people are relatives of Oisin's as there is a strong resemblance in most of them and they don't look much like Mick.

I'd have thought that Mick would be wrapped up in greeting people and wouldn't get a free moment to see us for a while. I couldn't have been more wrong. Making our way into the parlor, I can see that Mick is sat by himself in an armchair near the casket, not talking to anyone. He looks like he'd rather be huddled up in bed having a cry. The puffiness of his eyes suggests he's done rather a lot of that already.

As soon as Mick sees us come in, he gets up and hurries over to us. Marcus is the first one to him, and they hold onto one another for a long while. Tears slip down Mick's face, but neither he nor Marc says anything. After a few moments, Allen, Martin, and Jarrod step in to offer their support as well. They've all been in Mick's place before.

Freddie and Christian sort of stay aside, but still close enough to let Mick know they're there. The looks they exchange say it all—they know they're going to be there themselves one day and they don't really want to contemplate it. Clyde, Krist, and I sort of step away toward the casket. I've never been very easy with death and funerals, but Oisin looks quite natural really. I know it's a cliché, but he does look like he's just sleeping. He looks young and beautiful. Looking at him, I realize that this is the first time I've ever been to a funeral for someone who's died with HIV.

NATURALLY, the crowd is smaller at the committal service on Monday. From the group, it's just Jarrod, Allen, Marc, and I who go. A part of me wonders why I'm there; I didn't know Oisin, and I haven't gotten especially close to Mick. There's some need in me, though, to be there for one of the group that has done so much for me in such a short while.

On our way out of the cemetery Marc stops and says he'll catch us up in a couple minutes. Allen, Jarrod, and I continue on, but I glance back to see Marc sitting on the ground near a headstone. When Marcus joins up with us again, he seems calm and relaxed. Mick said he didn't feel up to going to the wake, though I got the impression that Oisin's family wasn't exactly warmly sympathetic toward Mick. Jarrod's going to drop us off at Willowmead and then go check on Mick.

Later in the afternoon, Trevor comes over to my flat. We're working on making dinner together when Trevor says that he thinks he's finally ready to go to Finley's grave, which is in the same cemetery as Oisin's committal. He doesn't want to go alone though, and asks if I would come with him. After considering it, I think I would be okay supporting him if he needs a mate, so I agree and we plan to go out there Thursday after breakfast.

I mention it to Jarrod when I have my appointment with him Tuesday. He reminds me that he's only a mobile ring away if Trevor or I need him as well, but he says he's quite proud of me being willing to go with Trevor. Sometimes a mate's support can do more than a counselor's, Jarrod always says. For as glad as I am that he's my psych doc, I do understand just what he means. There is no substitute for good mates.

Come Thursday, Trevor and I hop on a bus up the high road. We could have walked up; it probably only would have been forty-five minutes at an easy stroll, but neither of us want to push it too hard just yet. Besides, I'd want Trevor to take as much time as he needs once we get there. He seems to be doing well as we get off near the cemetery and start down the pathways, talking about how he and Finley used to go camping often.

"There was one time we were packing up to go, and I had a feeling that we were missing something, you know? So I mentioned it to Fin, and he said he was sure everything was fine, no worries. Only when we got to the campsite, it turned out we had no tent poles. We nearly had a blazing row over it until Fin made some comment about the poles in our trousers. We both started snickering and there was no staying mad after that. We just found a hotel and shagged each other rotten for the next three days."

Trevor's brilliant smile alone is worth coming out here. Reliving those good memories has to be a good thing for him, and I'm glad to be the one to share them with him. Then Trevor stops and his smile slips. He lets out a long breath, staring at the headstone in front of him. I take a half step back, I want to give him his space, but I don't want to be too far away either. Trevor doesn't seem to notice I'm there at all anymore.

He stands there, looking at the ground where the new grass is just beginning to come up, as if he can picture his boyfriend lying beneath the layer of earth. He seems calm at first glance, but looking closer you can see the tears. For a moment, I don't know what to say, but then I realize there isn't really anything I *can* say or do. I'm just here.

Trevor sits down on the ground, a lot like Marc did a few days ago. He reaches out and runs a hand over the new grass, and starts talking softly. I can't quite hear what he's saying, but I know it's not me he's talking to. I step a bit farther away, sitting under a nearby tree.

I try not to watch too much, I know this is a long-overdue good-bye that Trevor never got to have with Finley. I can't help thinking that I could be doing the same thing, only the one I need closure with isn't in the ground. In a way I feel like there's really no reason for me not to find Nick's contact information and ring him up. I don't feel ready though, and I know I need to work through a lot still. Or maybe I'm just clinging to hope… still.

After some while, Trevor gets up and comes to sit beside me. He looks tired and refreshed at the same time. We reach out for one another's hand and sit quiet for a while. Eventually we make our way back out of the cemetery to wait for the bus back down the high road.

"I think I need to do this again sometime," he says as we're heading back to Willowmead. "It hurt so much at first, but then I started talking to him and… I don't know, I guess that's what catharsis is."

At the meeting that evening, Marcus says he goes once a week to the cemetery to James' grave, and he offers to take Trevor with him any time he wants. After the funeral earlier in the week, death ended up being the topic of the evening. Jarrod tells the group that Mick's asked him to send his thanks for everyone's support and that he expects to be back with us before long. I hope he will be.

I HAVEN'T had any particularly odd dreams since the first night when I started on the meds, but that night after going to the cemetery with Trevor I have another one. I dream of being at Willowmead years on. I'm hanging about talking with mates, probably after the Thursday night group. Then out of nowhere, Nick comes to see me. He walks up and looks at me for a moment.

"I don't recognize you," he says, though he clearly knows it's me. I must look so different to him. He leans in, though, and tries to kiss me.

Then it all goes weird. As his lips touch mine I literally start to fall apart in his arms. First I'm too weak to make my lips respond to his, and then my body begins to disintegrate from under me.

Waking with a start, I feel myself to be sure I'm still solid and in one piece. I need a glass of water and, getting out of bed, I wonder if that dream isn't trying to tell me to lay off the idea of finding Nick. Maybe it was meant to be a warning that looking backward isn't helpful.

Later in the morning, I have a short appointment with Dr. Asha so she can explain the results from my blood tests. She says that the results are quite good, that it looks like the medication is working for me. My viral load is decreasing and my CD4 is a bit higher already.

I'm getting ready to go round to Marc and Freddie's for dinner with them and Archie that evening. I take a moment to look closely at myself in the mirror. I haven't paid all that much attention to my looks in the last few weeks. When I look, though, *really* look, I can see that I'm doing a lot better than I was when I first had a look at myself in that hospital mirror. I'm getting back to a healthy weight, looking a bit more in form, and my hair is starting to grow out. It'll be annoying when it gets to that awkward, in-between length though.

I can't help thinking about it: I've lived through something that I'm not sure even the worst people in the world should be subjected to, but I survived and I think I'm getting stronger, as a person, for it. There are good changes that have come to me despite the bad changes.

What amazes me the most is that it's all down to me. Well, me along with support from the best people I know. But it's me who's allowed the good changes to come. It's me who's survived and it's me who's stayed strong. It's me who did not and will not give up.

This is the best I've felt in months. I mean to do what I have to do to keep it that way for as long as I can.

CHAPTER 23

I HOPE I will be forgiven for not lingering too much over the next months. Life has become settled; things have sort of plateaued for me. If you think that's a bad thing, I could talk for England about how fucking great it feels. I am doing well and holding steady without much of a struggle. That's a lot more than I'd hoped for when all this started. Most of the time, I didn't think there *was* anything to hope for, even if I never gave up hoping.

I'm doing a lot to take care of myself. I haven't had any problems so far with my medication schedule. Once I got past the side effects, it hasn't been bad, and I'm rather well set in the routine by now. Those pills are my top priority. Other things help make a big difference too, though. Eating properly, for example. I keep meats to a minimum, and avoid anything that's quite processed. I've gotten a lot of good habits from Marc when it comes to diet.

When I started out, I was having an appointment with Jarrod each week and with Dr. Asha every other week. Now I see Jarrod every fortnight, other than at yoga and the Thursday meetings, and Dr. Asha once a month. She's said she anticipates cutting it back to seasonally because I'm doing so well.

Several times a month Geoff comes round for lunch, mostly just to be pleasant. Every so often he brings me an update on what he refers to as my "restitution." Through some vague references that he's let slip—usually after a couple lunch-hour Tanqueray and tonics—I've worked it out that the funds in my bank account, which are always there without any action on my part, have to do with the man from Form with the Glasgow grin. I'm not entirely sure how I feel about that, but I've gotten the impression that it'll be there no matter what I do, so I might as well accept it. I suppose there are a lot of things I don't know about what happened to me and perhaps it's best that I don't know any more than I do.

Spending time with my mates has also been good for me. I've found that they all have something unique to offer to my life. I'm not always sure just what it is that I have to offer them in return, but none of my mates have ever seemed burdened to have me around.

Marc and I often go to the yoga sessions on Mondays, and Trevor has started joining us regularly as well. Most Fridays I have dinner with Freddie and Marc, and usually Archie unless he's away on a buying trip. We've also started hanging out at Form again, usually Saturdays now. I don't drink very much at all, still, but sometimes I'll have something very light. I might nurse a lager almost all night. Krist is always at Form, at least for a while. Sometimes he stays around with us or decides to spend most of the night club-hopping, but only when he's in particularly *social* spirits. Usually if he hangs out at our table for any amount of time it's only to have a perch from which to scope his "prey."

Mick still lives at his flat, but he spends a lot of time at Willowmead now. He had a difficult time after losing Oisin, and he and I ended up becoming rather close. I think he found it really helpful to talk about his partner to someone who didn't know Oisin, who didn't have a friendship with him established before. Sometimes he wanted to be able to talk about things they argued about without feeling that he was betraying anyone's friendship or memory of Oisin. He's often told me since then that my being there for him was the best thing anyone did for him since he lost his "sunshine."

Then, of course, there are the Thursday evening meetings. I never really had much of a family. That was just one of those things that I had no frame of reference for. I feel differently now, though. Those who are a part of the Thursday group *are* my family, in the most real sense of the word. Even Archie has started sitting in with us occasionally because he wants to be more aware of and responsive to the circumstances Marc and I, and, to an extent, Freddie, deal with.

Other than Archie joining in, the biggest change the group has seen these last few months was the addition of a new member. It had been two new members for a few weeks, but... well, it still angers me to think about it.

Dave joined our group with his boyfriend Leyland a few months after Oisin's passing. I still can't say exactly what it was, but the first time I met them I knew something was off. I don't think I'm the only one who sensed it; there was a general feeling of trepidation that doesn't usually happen in our circle from the first time they sat down with us.

"Hello. We're a magnetic couple. I'm Leyland, he's Dave," Leyland said. "Dave was recently diagnosed positive," Leyland told us. "It seems there was a night of drunken revelry, and resulting alcohol-induced amnesia, that came back to haunt Dave years later," he said.

In fact, it's Leyland who told us just about everything about him and Dave. Dave was always dead quiet at the meetings. He'd hardly even look up when someone spoke to him, which I'd tried a number of times only to have Leyland answer for him or change the subject.

One time Krist asked Leyland straight out why he never let his boyfriend speak for himself. Leyland told Krist, in no uncertain terms, that Dave had been through quite enough already without having to answer questions about things people ought not to be asking someone in his state. Krist didn't like that answer at all, and it was the only time I'd ever heard a raised voice from Jarrod as he tried to keep the peace.

The week after that incident, Dave was at the meeting without his "interpreter." At first he was as quiet as he was before, but after a few of us talked for a bit, Dave started to open up. And once he started, he couldn't stop. I don't think any of us were entirely surprised by what he told us, but we were all shocked and some of us were feeling a bit vindictive by the time he finished his story.

That week, Dave had been looking for his mobile and thought maybe Leyland had mistaken it for his (again) and had it in his laptop case. When he went to check, he found a bottle of pills as well and thought maybe his boyfriend had picked up his HAART meds for him. Only it was *Leyland's* name on the label. Dave rang the chemist to let them know there was a mistake, but he was told that there was no mistake and that Leyland had had that same prescription for the last five years.

Dave had only met Leyland three years ago.

He realized at once what was going on and also realized that Leyland had been controlling and manipulating him for a long time. Dave left him immediately and came directly to Willowmead. He hasn't left. Leyland is a long-term guest of Her Majesty's Prison Service.

Fortunately, Dave is doing a lot better now. He's still relatively quiet most of the time, but he does manage to get chatty after a coffee. I haven't failed to notice the attention Archie pays Dave whenever he's tagging along with us.

I no longer live at Willowmead.

I had been there for over a year when one night, during dinner at theirs, Marc asked me if I'd consider taking their apartment. Freddie had just recently received a big promotion and rise, and also a new office closer to the city proper, and they had started to think about looking for a place closer to town as well. Then what Marc said really left me gobsmacked—he said he wanted me to *have* the place, not to sell it to me. I laughed at first and asked if he was completely cracked, but he gave me this dead serious headshake. It was his place with Jamey, and he's finally feeling that he's ready to leave it, but he still doesn't want just anyone living here. It would mean a lot to him to know the right person was here.

I gave it some thought for a couple days and then spent another few days talking about it with just about everybody—Jarrod, Dr. Asha, Geoff, even Krist and Trevor. Finally I agreed to take it, though I still felt somewhat like I was *taking* something from Marc and Freddie. Of course when they found their gorgeous new place and took me round to see it before they moved, I didn't feel quite so bad.

I still spend a fair bit of time at Willowmead, I'm just a stroll away. It was a little tough at first, getting used to really being in my own place again. I was entirely independent at Willowmead, of course, but the way things are there it's more like a hotel than anything. I was used to having anything I needed on-site. Now I've got to cross the park for Monday yoga and the Thursday meeting, instead of just going downstairs. And my mates aren't just two doors down where I can pop round for tea and a chat whenever I feel like it. I've gotten adjusted, though, and it is a good step for me.

Now whenever Freddie is out of town, Marcus comes over to his old place to stay with me. We are a pair of nutters when left to our own devices. Marc is a good influence in some things, not so much in others. We do a lot of staying up past our bedtimes, watching action movies with little-to-no plot, and—would I make this up—prank phone calls. Apparently that was Marc's specialization as a kid back in California. I didn't get the humor of it at first, ringing up some random number and ringing off as soon as the poor sod on the other end answered, but after watching Marc do it a few times and crack up every time, I think it started rubbing off on me. Infectious laughter, I suppose. One thing's true, we are more like prepubescent boys than grown men sometimes.

There's one particular week in October, more than two years after I woke in hospital to find my life changed forever. Marc is staying with me for a few days. We're just sitting about one afternoon watching movies. I decide to make a quick run down to the market to pick up a few things for dinner while Marc is going for a shower. He says it looks like rain, and I promise him I'll be quick and lock the flat on my way out so that Norman Bates can't get to him. Well, that's what happens when you admit having been terrified by *Psycho*.

It doesn't take me long at the shop, but I can tell by the way the wind is picking up that I'll need to hurry home to beat the rain. I hurry back out onto South Leigh and turn toward home with a quick wave to the shop owner, who's always exceptionally nice to me.

I haven't gotten very far when I hear behind me, maybe half a block away, a tentative question.

"Padrig?"

I stop dead in my tracks and don't turn straight away. I hadn't thought I'd ever hear that voice speak my name again. I have to take a moment to ask myself if I'm certain I'm not just dreaming. I even press my thumbnail into my forefinger to see if I can feel it. I swallow hard when I turn round and see just a few yards away those warm brown eyes that were always able to make me feel all melty inside.

CHAPTER 24

"NICK?"

My voice comes out in a tiny whisper. I hardly dare to believe I'm looking at him and not hallucinating. He doesn't look very different; his hair is shorter, and he looks a little older than three years should have done to him. His hair is a bit lighter at the temples, and maybe there are some little lines around his eyes that I don't remember being there before. He's still bloody gorgeous; I knew he always would be.

I guess he's taking stock, too, because he hasn't said anything more. I'm starting to feel a bit awkward, us standing on the pavement just looking at one another after all this time. Nick takes a breath and opens his mouth to say something, but he's interrupted by a big gust of wind and rain pelting down upon us.

"Oh shit," I mumble. "Come on!" I grab for Nick's arm and start running back toward the flat. I feel sorry for Nick; he has no idea what's going on. By the time we're halfway back, we're both soaked anyway. I start laughing and can't help myself, we're drenched, must look like two drowned rats. Nick starts laughing too. It must be that infectious laughter again. By the time we get into the building we're dripping wet and out of breath.

"Fuck… well now I'm really sorry," he pants, leaning against the newel post and grinning slightly.

I swallow hard realizing how much I've missed that uneven grin. It takes me a couple shots at getting the key in the lock before I get the door open. "Come on, I'll get us some towels," I say, locking the door behind us again. Marc is still in the shower, I can hear him moaning over the sound of the running water. I think he misses the shower more than anything about this place. I have to hand it to James, a water heater and shower pressure most Brits only see in the movies, all for his Californian boyfriend.

I dry off in my bedroom and change out of my wet clothes before taking a towel back to Nick, still stood in the entryway, and telling him I've a dressing gown for him on my bed, second door back. I'll put some tea on and then put his things in the dryer for him. He nods and goes back toward my room, but doesn't say anything.

This is about to get awkward. The shock is starting to wear off, and it's beginning to hit me that I've just run into my ex-boyfriend, who I haven't seen in almost three years because of a bad situation, and now he's here in my apartment, changing into my clothes. How the hell am I going to say everything that needs to be said? Do I even know what needs to be said, and what *doesn't*?

Nick steps into the kitchen in my burgundy dressing gown before I have a chance to sort it out. It looks as if neither of us knows what to say next. Fortunately, the kettle does and spares us an awkward start for a few more moments. Pouring out two mugs, I can't help thinking this little scene is so domestic that if anyone walked in right now, they'd have no idea of the gulf of space and time that stands between Nick and me.

So, quite naturally, that's exactly when someone does walk in.

"Didn't I tell you you'd get caught in—" Marc's smirk freezes when he sees Nick there. Not that he knows Nick is Nick, of course. "Sorry, I didn't know you had anybody over." Marc is easy to read: he's wondering how the hell I found someone to shag that fast, and wondering if he doesn't know me half as well as he thinks he does.

"It's alright, mate. You were right, the skies opened up on us out there. Marc, I'd like you to meet Nick."

Again I can read his look, brief as it is—"*that* Nick?" his wide eyes ask.

"Hey, nice to meet you," he says, offering his hand to Nick. "I'll be in my room, okay, Pad?" I know what he means there too. "You know where to find me if you want to talk."

"Okay."

Nick sits down at the kitchen table where I've sat a mug of orange pekoe for him. I sit across the table. For a moment Nick stares into his tea before he glances up. "Boyfriend?" he asks quietly.

God... I missed his voice. That gentle, low tone; he always spoke so calmly.

I shake my head. "Nah, Marc is a mate. Freddie's boyfriend, actually."

Nick gives a puff of wry laughter. "Last time I spoke to Fred I think he wanted to rip my throat out."

Probably. We're both quiet for a moment. We both know this is it. I can tell the words "I'm sorry" are on the tip of his tongue, but don't want to hear it yet. I need to know other things first.

"What brought you to South Leigh?" I ask, trying to sound casual.

He hasn't quite met my eyes since we stood there on the pavement staring at one another. Now he's rubbing subconsciously at the back of his neck like he always did when he was feeling nervous.

"I don't know," he says quietly. "Well, I mean, I did come down here to have a look at the bookstore on the corner. I've heard the owner is thinking of selling and wanted to see it before talking about anything. I didn't really feel like going straight there though." He shrugs. "I was just wondering what the fuck I was doing, wandering aimlessly under threat of rain, when... I thought I saw you come out of that market. Guess I did."

"I thought you'd gone back to the States." I try to sound politely curious, like it hasn't been burning in me for the last couple years.

He nods, takes a sip of tea. "Yeah. I went back for a while. I just got back here a few weeks ago. It's... been a long couple years. There've been a lot of changes."

"Yeah," I agree. "Why did you decide to come back?"

"Because I never really left," Nick says. "I mean, I left, but I wasn't really there, you know? Even the things that were working were just... incomplete when I was back there. I was.... You remember I was cutting back on drinking for a while?"

He glances up slightly and I nod.

"I started again, after you left. I didn't realize how bad it was until I went back to the States. I had myself pretty screwed up for a while. I lost my job here because of the drinking. Mr. Soames passed away and the new barrister didn't give a toss about my case records when he figured out I was hungover every bloody morning and drinking at lunch. Things got to be too much, so I went back there for a while. I got help that time, though, getting myself back on track. I really made some changes in my life, stopped kidding myself about things. I started writing again, you know? Some of my stuff has been published and it's... done pretty well. Even met somebody."

I wonder if he notices my flinch when he says that.

"Anyway, getting around to your question...." He always rambled like that. "That's why I came back here. Don knew about what happened to us and he was the one who.... You know, a few months ago he just said to me one day that as much as he cared for me, he knew I couldn't be happy, really, there with him. I knew he was right. If nothing else, I needed to come here again and to at least try to talk to you again."

We're both quiet for a moment, again. I realize this isn't going to go anywhere unless I talk too. It's been long enough, I'm ready to do this now. I think.

"I've thought about trying to find you as well," I say. "At first I was thinking of flying to New York, but... I kind of ran into some roadblocks and, to be honest, I think I lost my bottle. Though it was also because I realized I needed to take care of myself for a while too."

Nick looks up at me properly, finally. I see in his eyes the understanding that we've *both* had to do a lot of work on ourselves. He's been there and can tell I have too.

"Padrig. I've needed for a long time to talk to you about that night. You deserve to know what really happened."

CHAPTER 25

I RESIST the impulse to hold my breath and brace myself. I have to remind myself not to jump to the conclusions that I've held onto all this time. Nick's got to have his day in court, as it were.

He takes a long breath, and I can tell he's thinking the same as me, that it's been long enough; it's time to clear the air. "That conference I went to that week, it was such a waste of time for me. I was realizing at that time how much I really disliked my work, and I wished I'd have just blown it off and gone with you on holiday. Once it all wrapped up that Saturday night, I went to a pub with some colleagues, figured I'd just have the one to be friendly.

"I was about halfway through my pint when somebody else at the bar started making conversation. We were just talking about the cricket match that was on the telly, nothing deep or particularly interesting. I didn't want to be there anyway and definitely had no interest in that guy. Then I started feeling sleepy. I figured it was just that it had been a tough week for me, but this guy said he was going to ring himself a cab anyway and he'd be happy to share. I gave him the address, but apparently I passed out before getting home. I still remember nothing between getting in the cab and waking up Sunday with a stranger beside me.

"I had no idea what was going on and the guy asked me if my housemate knew I slept with men because he looked offended when he saw us in bed. I just didn't know how I could have ever gotten so drunk I'd bring anybody back, let alone this guy who was nowhere near my type. He was really big, built, kind of scary-looking, beady-eyed. I was almost hysterical when I told him to get out, but he didn't seem bothered at all. I remember watching him going down toward the park, talking on his mobile with this unnerving grin on his face.

"Well… I tried ringing you after that. You had every right to leave for what you saw, I know that, but I just wanted you to know that I didn't do anything like that on purpose. I would never have done that to you." He's so quiet by the time he stops. It must be like reliving it for him; I know I've done that enough times myself.

I think I'm starting to put things together here. It's all too similar to be coincidence.

"He put something in your drink, didn't he?" I ask Nick.

Nick nods. "I found out that afternoon. I decided I needed to go to a clinic as soon as I could. I didn't know what else to do. I was feeling pretty awful, physically I mean, not just emotionally. They told me there was Rohypnol in my system, but there wasn't any sign that he'd… you know, done anything. I gave the police a description, but nothing ever came of it. I think they ignored me on purpose."

"Alex is dead," I murmur. Nick stares at what seems like a grim non sequitur. It had to be. It all fits too well to have been anyone else. I just wonder *why*…. Guess it's my turn. "I've got a lot to tell you about as well."

Nick moves to reach for my hand, but he hesitates and stops. I know what he's feeling. It's been three years, now here we are again and there are some habits and feelings that haven't changed. He wants to hold my hand, to reassure me. And I want him to. But neither of us is certain that we *should*. Nick just nods for me to go on.

"I guess you found my bag by the door?"

"Yeah, when I threw that guy out. I was really hoping you'd be back when you calmed down, or I could find you at Fred's."

"I should have been there. I… I ended up running down to the park and having a cry. I thought I'd just go to Freddie's and cool down and eventually we'd have to talk. I still regret that I ran out the way I did. Had I just talked to you, none of this would have happened."

"You couldn't help reacting, Pad," Nick says gently. "When you didn't answer your phone, I tried Fred's. He said he hadn't seen you and all he'd got was an upset text message from you. He was... um... seriously angry with me and wouldn't listen to my side."

"Freddie's like that."

"Thing is, I really thought you were there with him and he was covering for you. I would have understood it, I was just worried sick. I got your message saying you weren't coming back, but I needed to know you weren't... well, obviously you were hurt, you wouldn't not have been, but.... Fuck, I was so scared you were going to jump off a bridge or something. I needed to know where you were. Even if you were with someone else, I just wanted to know you were safe."

Fuck that shit about not being sure if we should touch. I need to hold Nick's hand, right now, and I don't doubt he'll need it too once I get this out. I put my hand over his and curl my fingers in just a bit. "Nick. What I need to tell you, 'hard' doesn't cover it. I've been wondering for a long time how I would tell you this, or if I even could do it. I don't know how you'll react."

"It's okay, Padrig," he says, contrary to the concern I see in the set of his features.

"I never made it to Freddie's. There weren't any bridges involved. I told you I was having a cry in the park. I was really vulnerable right then, you know? I just wanted to be left alone, but some guy came along and offered me a cup of tea when he saw me crying. I ended up following along with him just to appease him. I figured I'd just have one cup and be off to call in all Freddie's favors at once."

There's sadness in Nick's eyes, and I can tell he's guessed a part of what happened. I also know he can't possibly know how much worse it got. I hate doing this, hate telling him what happened and seeing the hurt I've dealt with myself reflected in his eyes. I never wanted to cause him hurt, especially now that I'm almost 100 percent sure that this is all connected and he didn't do anything to hurt me. We both need this though; it's a long-since-due healing.

"I passed out after drinking that one cup. I woke up feeling really horrid, and sore."

Nick shuts his eyes tightly, and I don't know if I can tell him the rest. I swear this hurts more than living it did. "There's a lot more, Nick. If you don't want me to tell you right now…."

"It's not going to hurt less later."

He's right. Soldier on. "I was locked in. They kept me like that, two of them. One of them was a big, scary guy with beady eyes. I never sent any of the messages anyone received from me. I was on drugs most of the time, I don't even know what exactly. They… made a lot of money from me."

I wait a moment, trying to gauge Nick's reaction so far. It was one of the first things I worried about, telling Nick what had happened to me. He's staring down at our hands, not quite clasped, with his head bowed. I've never seen him cry before. "Nick?"

He nods, telling me it's okay to go on. "You got out, though?" he whispers, a faint note of hope in that pained sound.

"Yes, someone helped me. He got me out and took me to hospital. I know next to nothing about him, just that he's my guardian angel, of a sort."

"Thank god he helped you," Nick whispers.

"At least I got to go through the withdrawal without remembering most of it. I know it wasn't very comfortable, but I was pretty much disconnected. It was almost a week before I really came out of it enough to talk to the doctors."

And this is what I hate more than anything to hit Nick with, what comes next. I know what it's like to think the worst is over, only to be told there's more. At this point, it's harder for others to hear than for me to say. I've reached acceptance. I know the only thing you can do is be honest, but gentle.

But, fuck, I don't want him to reject me. I don't want to hear him say, "Padrig, I'm sorry for everything. But I can't."

I can't not tell him, though. If there's any shot, no matter how remote, he has to know. Now. At the moment I'm not thinking of what he said, that he met someone over there.

"They told me they ran a few different tests when I was brought in, because of the situation. Most of them were okay, but I tested positive for HIV."

Nick takes a long, stuttering breath, lowering his head even further. Now he does grasp my hand, so tightly it almost hurts. I know he needs to let it out, but I have to tell him I'm doing all right. I get up and come round to his side of the table, sitting beside him and keeping our hands joined.

"It's okay," I say softly, meaning both of us. I'm okay, and it's okay for him to cry.

"Padrig...." He stops, not knowing what to say, or not able.

"It's alright, l-ove." Yeah, I'd started to catch myself there, but then realized there was no reason to. I've loved him all along, haven't I?

"It's just... Pad, I didn't know. I was so scared something bad had happened, but I didn't *know*. Pad, you're the last person in the world who should've.... I feel like it's my fault, I should've—"

"Nick, it's not your fault. You didn't have anything to do with what happened. I think it was all something that was done to both of us by evil people, though I don't know why. You're not guilty of anything."

Nick is quiet for a long moment.

"I came back here to tell you I'm sorry, because I've been hiding for long enough and I knew we both needed some kind of closure. I didn't expect anything, I just knew I had to try to find you, and I hoped you'd listen. I didn't think you should have to live with thinking I didn't love you. I'm sorry for not doing it sooner, but... maybe it wasn't the right time for either of us."

"It likely wouldn't have been," I agree. "It's taken me a while to get to where I am, but I'm doing well. I'm actually healthier now than I've ever been, I think. In all ways."

"You look really well. I'm glad you're okay. I think I'm better now as well, now that I'm *me*. I gave up the legal career after I lost my job, but it was probably one of the best things that could have happened. I wasn't happy with it, never was. I was trying to be something I wasn't."

"I know you were, I'm glad you're doing something good for you now."

"Dad wasn't very happy. I knew he wouldn't be. His gay, paralegal son coming 'home' a drunken wreck. He passed away about a year and a half ago."

"I'm sorry, Nick."

I knew Nick and his father didn't have the best relationship. I always figured it was why Nick decided he wanted to move back here to go to university. His father was a barrister who took a job in New York City and moved the family there when Nick was only three. Nick was back here every summer on holidays though and has always called Blighty his *home*. Nick went to university to study law, like his dad wanted, but he ended up deciding that he could never have a "barrister's voice" in court and decided to switch to studying for a paralegal degree. It was a compromise; Nick *really* always wanted to be a writer.

"Turns out having a fry-up five mornings out of seven actually *is* unhealthy," Nick says with a half-shrug. "I had no idea what kind of estate dad had until I read the will. It was… rather tidy. That's when I decided I was done with law and started writing. It's gone a lot better than I expected."

"That's really good to hear." I smile, but if anyone looked really closely they'd find it's bittersweet. I'd forgotten when I was telling him, but it's come back to me now. "I'll bet your boyfriend's a proud bloke to have you."

"I don't think Don qualifies as my boyfriend anymore. We split before I came back here. Mutually. He understood that I couldn't share my heart when… well, because I've never…." Nicks sighs and glances away. "I'm trying feebly to say that I still love you. So much it hurts. I always have, think I always will."

My heart leaps in my chest and does a somersault. I can't spare a thought to poor Don; the hope that I would one day hear Nick say that was the only thing that kept me from giving up more times than I could count.

"I know everything is different, we've both been through so much. I'll understand if it's not the same for you. I just want to be able to talk to you again, more than anything."

I squeeze Nick's hand gently. "I have been through a lot, yeah. And I've changed, greatly."

"I know, and I understand...."

"Nick, how I *feel* hasn't changed though. I never stopped loving you either. Even when every time I thought of you I thought you'd cheated. I always figured that made me a first-class prat, but I couldn't help it."

There's a long, deep silence between us, and I think Nick's waiting for his heart to finish its gymnastics as well.

"What does this mean?" he asks cautiously.

"I don't really know. I think, maybe, we have a lot to process before we can answer that."

"Yeah, you're probably right," Nick says. I can tell he's a bit disappointed, even if he does agree.

If I'm really honest with myself, I can't see us not trying it again at some point, but there's just no way I can jump into that. I've got to have a think, a long one, and sort out some things. Then I've got to have a chat with a few people. When it comes to it, we really are starting over. If that's what we're doing.

"Do you want to get dressed?" I ask, slowly letting go of his hand. We need a little space.

Nick nods and goes to get his things from my washer-dryer in the cupboard outside the bath. He doesn't take long. I'm clearing our tea mugs when he comes back into the kitchen. He's looking out the window at the lowering sun that's poking through the last of the clouds. "I should probably think about getting home."

"Okay. Can I ring you?"

"Yeah, of course. Let me give you my mobile."

I take mine from the kitchen table and put him in my contacts, then ring it right away so he can save mine as well.

"Thanks," Nick says. "Thank you." I know he doesn't mean about the mobile.

I step close to give him a hug, wondering if it's not going to be a bit awkward. It is, but for only second, and then it feels just like it always did holding him—*right*. We still fit together just the same.

"I'm so glad you've come back, Nick," I say.

"Me too," he says in a quiet, choked voice. I hold him a little tighter for a while longer, giving him a chance to wipe away his tears before he pulls back.

We walk over to the front door. Nick says, "Have a good night," for lack of anything else to say I guess.

"You as well. Be careful getting home, yeah?"

"Yeah." He always did that, echoed me.

Before he steps out into the corridor, he leans in and brushes his lips against my cheek, missing the corner of my lips by only a hair. He turns and I watch him go down the stairs and out the door.

I have a lot of thinking to do.

CHAPTER 26

"PAD?" I hear Marc say tentatively as he comes into the kitchen. I've put on another pot and nod toward it. Marc's been a transplant long enough to know what I mean. He pours himself a cup and sits down across from me at the table. He doesn't need to ask anything.

"I just can't believe it. For so long I didn't think I'd ever see him again, no matter how much I kept hoping. And then he's just *there*, on bloody South Leigh."

"Yeah, probably a pretty big surprise. Was he looking for you?"

"Kind of. That's why he came back here. It had to be coincidence, though, him being on South Leigh. I'm ex-directory."

"How did it go?"

"We're going to keep in touch. I think we both have a lot to think over. I told him everything that happened, but I feel like we still have a lot to talk about."

Marc nods. "What did he say?"

"Well, he said he…." Without warning I feel tears rushing up. I kept it together the whole time talking with Nick, but now I break down. I haven't cried like this since I first moved into Willowmead.

It hits me all at once, everything Nick said comes together. Bennett and Alex targeted him as well. Why they wanted us, I can't begin to know. They had to have been very detailed, knowing when I was away and when I'd be back. When I think of that bastard Alex with my Nick….

I can remember it, getting home and seeing that man in our bed. I hadn't put it together until Nick described him. The room was dark and I didn't spend very long scrutinizing, but that big, scary-looking guy could only have been Alex.

Marc gets up and comes to sit close so he can hug me. "Come on, Pad, let's sit in the living room, okay? You'll be more comfortable."

I let Marc walk me over to the couch, and we just sit there for a long time.

"It was them, it was Alex," I say eventually, my voice a little raw. "He's the one who was in bed with Nick that morning. Nick said he went to the clinic that afternoon and was told he'd been given Rohypnol. It's like they wanted to get us both."

"Whoa," Marcus breathes. That sums it up.

"I think Nick wants to be together again." I need to move the focus for a moment. "Even though I told him I'm poz. Maybe it just didn't sink in right away, I don't know. I was always so scared he wouldn't want me if I told him that."

"Anybody who would react that way isn't worthy of anyone's affection, Pad, let alone yours. Fact is, when it's really love, there's no illness or handicap that can deter it. In fact, sometimes it makes the love stronger. How are you feeling, though?"

"I still love him, Marc. There's no doubt of that. I need some time though, to get used to the idea again. I can't... can't just do this all at once. I need to know things won't be all wrong if we try it again. I want it so much though. I've wanted nothing but for him to hold me and tell me he still loved me for three years now. I've waited this long, though, I really don't want to mess it now."

"You won't mess anything up, Pad. Of course you need time to adjust, you both do. And you know I'm with you, right? All of us are."

"Thanks, Marc. I'm gonna need to talk to Jarrod as well."

Marc nods. "I can call him for you, if you want."

"I'd appreciate that. Not straight away though, I want to have a lie down for a bit. Just want to rest and think on my own."

"Okay. You want me to cook up some supper? Maybe I'll see if Jarrod can come eat with us."

"That would be alright. You're a good mate, one of the best."

Marc smiles and squeezes my shoulders. "Go ahead and get some rest, Pad. Don't be worried about anything. I'll take care of whatever comes up."

I get up and go back to my bedroom. My dressing gown is folded neatly by my pillow. Picking it up, I'm about to lose it again. Lying down, I hold onto the dressing gown like a security blanket, like I want to hold Nick.

The only thing I can think of is the time Nick and I met. I was at a little pub with Freddie and Archie. We used to go there sometimes before going to Form. We'd had our first round there that night, and the whole time I couldn't take my eyes off this bloke sitting at the bar.

He was wearing a fitted light-gray suit, and his handsome profile looked tired. I got the impression he'd had a tough day at work. I wanted to go over and talk to him, but I wasn't quite brave enough. Archie went to the bar to get us another round, and I was mortified when I saw him say something to the guy in gray and gesture back toward our table. Then Nick smiled at me and I was done.

Nick took one of the glasses from Archie and picked up his own to come join us. I had no idea what I was going to say. Nick just set the fresh pint he was carrying in front of me and sat down saying, "Hi," like we were old friends.

I was blushing when I mumbled, "Hello."

"It's been such a shitful week," Nick said. "But when your friend told me you've been checking me out the whole time you've been here, well... that made me feel really good. I'm Nick, by the way, really nice to meet you." He held out his hand.

"Padrig," I said, offering my hand in return. Only he didn't shake it; he held it tenderly for a moment before kissing it. I didn't think I could blush more, but I was wrong.

We went out together the next evening, and everything was just so... right. I could never have imagined then that we'd be here, more than four years later, having to start all over again.

I've had enough lying in bed and decide to take a shower.

By the time I'm cleaned up and dressed again, I can hear Marc shifting pots and pans, running taps, and talking to Jarrod. I guess I'm going to be doing this, telling people about Nick being back, more than a few times.

"Hey, Pad," Jarrod says with a smile when I walk into the kitchen. I know that smile, the one that says, "I don't know exactly what's up, but I'm ready to listen whenever you want."

"Hey, Jarrod," I say, sitting down beside him at the table. I sound tired even to my own ears.

"Tea?" Marc asks. "Dinner will be ready in about ten or fifteen."

"Yeah, that'd be great."

"Love some. Thanks, Marc," Jarrod says.

Only hours ago it was Nick and I sitting across from one another with tea, for the first time in years.

"You're never going to believe this."

CHAPTER
27

"I'D BE more than happy to meet you and Nick at some point," Jarrod says as we're moving into the lounge after dinner. I've told him just about everything Nick told me and that I think it's all connected. "You could definitely invite him to the Thursday meeting as well. I think you're taking this quite healthily, Padrig. I understand it's a bit of a shake-up, but it sounds like your considerations are very level-headed—taking things slowly, giving yourself, and Nick, the time and space to think, and, of course, talking about it."

I grin at him. "I've had a good counselor."

"One who's away in the head, anyway. How are you feeling, overall?"

"I don't know, I think I'm a bit conflicted, really. When I think about it, when I think that those two actually must have targeted both Nick and I, and that they wanted to cause us hurt and knew just how to do it.... I don't understand it, and it makes me mad. But in a way, I'm relieved as well, to know that Nick didn't just go to bed with someone else. I don't like saying it, but I think it actually makes me feel a little better, knowing it wasn't *just* me they were after."

"I know what you mean," Jarrod nods. "I'm thinking you might consider talking to Krist about some of the angry feelings you're experiencing, since the two of you have some common ground."

"Yeah, I'll want to have a chat with a few of the guys. You really wouldn't mind if I invited Nick to the meeting Thursday?"

"He's more than welcome to join us."

"Maybe we could have lunch or something before the meeting, the three of us?"

Jarrod smiles. "That was going to be my next suggestion."

A deep yawn slips out of me, and Jarrod squeezes my shoulder. "I know when I'm boring my audience. You try and get some rest tonight, alright, Pad? Don't hesitate to ring me anytime. Let me know about lunch."

After Jarrod takes off, Marc and I sit on the couch for a while. I've switched to have a cup of chamomile-lavender tea; that's usually soothing. It's nice to just sit with Marc, not having to talk about anything. That's what I need at the moment. Tomorrow I'll go round and talk to Krist, maybe I'll stop in and see Trevor as well. Freddie will be back Wednesday afternoon, I'll definitely talk to him and Archie then. Nick was their friend as well, after all.

By morning, I'm feeling okay. Maybe I'd been becoming emotionally complacent; things have been going so smoothly for me, personally, that I've probably been doing more to help others through their rough spots than I've needed to do for myself. When I think about it, I'm not sure I'm ever going to come to the same level of acceptance about being drugged and prostituted that I have about my HIV status. But having that situation opened again makes me see how far I've come in being able to deal with it.

I'm tempted to ring Nick, but I decide to go round to Krist's for a while first. I don't want to seem like I'm being too quick about things. On my way into Willowmead, I go through the west wing's English garden. The plants are all going dormant for winter, but it's still comforting and calming. It's a nice day, not too chilly, and the sun's peeking through. I wish I could hear the autumn leaves scratching down the walkways and being crunched as I go, but that rain last night left everything damp.

Upstairs, it takes Krist a few minutes to open his door, and when he does he looks a bit rough.

"Pad-babe. Woke me up," he mumbles, pulling me into his flat.

"Sorry about that." Yeah, right. It's already noon, and sleeping that late on a Tuesday just seems... decadent. I make myself comfortable on his couch. There's no need of pleasantries between us.

"Before you say it, I am fine, *not* hungover. I was out late dancing. Fun is not restricted to Friday and Saturday, you know."

Ah, Krist, don't ever change!

"So then... you look like you are here for something particular. Something is on your mind. I can always tell when you are thinking a lot. You pout. Not that it is unattractive; it is very adorable on you."

Krist never minces words, so I won't either. "I ran into Nick yesterday afternoon."

Krist goes from hungover to wide awake in about three seconds. "Are you serious?" he says, sitting down beside me on his couch. "Just ran into him, out of the blue?"

I nod.

"What was he doing back here?" There's an apprehensive tone in Krist's question.

"Think he said something about looking at that bookstore up on South Leigh, but ultimately he wanted to find me."

Krist raises a brow, waiting for the story.

"What he told me... I'm still trying to process it."

"Talk to me, Pad-babe," he says, pulling me close and wrapping his arms around me.

"That morning, when I found him in bed. What he told me yesterday... it was Alex who was in bed with him."

"You mean he was with...." Krist slowly sits up straight and says to me in all seriousness, "If he was with *that* man, Padrig, I know a thousand ways to kill a person."

"No, Krist, you don't understand. Nick wasn't *with* them, they were after him as well as me. He said he'd just been talking about the cricket with somebody at the pub the night before and then started feeling sleepy. Nick said he went to the clinic the next day and was told someone had used Rohypnol on him. Krist... all this time I've thought he didn't love me like I loved him. That was probably exactly what those fuckers wanted me to think."

Krist has gone back to holding me and rubbing my shoulder. "They wanted to hurt your Nick, and get to you," he says thoughtfully.

"They succeeded."

"But they did not win, Padrig. Here you are. They are not."

"Yeah. You know, I've thought I've dealt with it pretty well the last couple years. I've moved on with my life, you know? But when I think about them hurting Nick.... I could deal with what they did to me, but I'm *angry* about them having hurt him."

"Let me know when you get to the point of wanting to punch a hole in their chest to tear out their hearts. That was how I felt when I was discharged. Or you can try imaging their *Eier* stuck in a fish bowl. Only replace the goldfish with a piranha."

He's not talking about scrambled or fried. I've gotten used to Krist's phraseology over the years. I can say all manner of filthy things in German. "Have I ever told you, you belong in an institution, mate? Society at large isn't ready for Kristof Anders," I tell him with a grin.

"They never will be, Pad-babe. This is the curse of the unique and honest. We are too *fantastisch* for common people to contemplate. You can call on my superpowers anytime. I will listen, help you dream of new torture ideas, make you laugh, and then you will feel all better."

"Glad I know you, Krist. I don't think I'd have come half as far without you."

"I never imagined I would know anyone in a similar situation." He actually sounds serious for once. "You are a good influence on me. You noticed I said I was not hungover this morning."

"Yeah, I did check that. Quite an improvement. Starting on a HAART regimen next as well?"

Krist gives a sarcastic laugh. "I would not get my hopes up, were I you. Now, what are you doing sitting here cuddling me when you should be catching up with Nick? And also, when will I meet him?"

"I'm going to ring him when I get home. I'm hoping he'll come to the meeting Thursday. We'll see. I don't want him to feel pushed or pressured or anything. Well, I wanted to stop in and talk to Trev before I get back home, so…."

Krist shakes his head though. "Let him sleep. He was out last night as well. You already interrupted *my* beauty sleep."

"Maybe you ought to try an induced coma," I say, pulling a face.

"Fuck you," Krist says, sounding bored. "I know I am the prettiest one here. And so do you." He leans in and kisses me full on the mouth. That's just Krist.

"Okay, well, maybe I'll just talk to him at the meeting. See you then, yeah?"

Krist just smiles and sees me out. I wonder about him and Trevor having been "out" late. Trevor has come a really long way since he first came to Willowmead. He gets out quite a bit, though not as much as Krist. I wonder if maybe there's something developing between the two of them. I could give Krist a damn good ragging if I found out he's gone back on his own vow against love.

I do ring Nick when I get home. We make plans to have lunch here again tomorrow and to talk more then.

I held myself back from ringing on the walk over from Willowmead, waiting till I got back in. Hope has been growing in me ever since we had our chat yesterday, and I know me: once I start hoping I can get a little carried away if I don't watch it. Too much of that can lead to disappointment. When I was younger I used to try to tell myself it was better just not hoping at all. That never really worked, though, and hope has gotten me through some very dark moments. Still, this time I find myself not wanting to hope for too much too soon. I cannot rush things with Nick; we are more or less starting over from scratch.

CHAPTER 28

I'M PREPARING lunch Wednesday afternoon when the bell rings. Marc lets Nick in, and I can't help thinking of Nick mistaking Marc for my boyfriend the other day. It's usually Trevor or Krist people think I'm with, though Nick hasn't met them yet, and most people think Krist is *with* everybody. Mostly because he has been.

From the kitchen doorway, Nick says, "Hi," before Marc ushers him in and offers something to drink from my fridge. Marc still acts like he's the host when he's round. I don't mind at all; I know this was his place for years. I even asked him if he wanted me to keep one of the pictures of him and Jamey on the mantle when I moved in. I thought it would be kind of nice to keep something of their "spirit" here, and Marc was deeply touched by that.

Marc pours us all a ginger ale, and he and Nick sit at the kitchen table, chatting about growing up on either coast of the States. They seem to be getting on really well, and I'm relieved about that. There aren't many people Marc doesn't get on with though; he's a very open person.

I bring three salads over. I made a fresh loaf of bread as well and put some warm slices in a basket on the table. "There's pepper steak soup in the pot being kept warm whenever you lads are ready for it," I tell them, sitting beside Marc, across from Nick.

"Pad makes the best soups," Marc says.

"You don't have to tell me, I always loved it when he'd make soup. Especially in the fall." Nick smiles a sort of wistful smile. I remember a few times when I had a day off and would make a pot of soup for supper. Nick always acted like it was the best thing I could have done for him when he got home.

I wonder if Nick is getting the same sensation of *pull* between us that I am just now. We used to be unable to keep our hands off one another. Not necessarily in a sexual way, we were just always touching, in contact with one another. We held hands a lot. Even while eating. Nick's right-handed but has always eaten with his left hand, for some reason. It meant we could hold hands across the table. Yeah, we were one of *those* couples, a pair of complete saps. Our hands are close to touching already by the time we've finished lunch.

Marc excuses himself to go pack up his bag. Freddie's home today and will be by around suppertime to pick Marc up.

"Lunch was excellent," Nick says. "You were always great in the kitchen."

I can't believe I blush at that. It isn't the compliment but a memory of us fucking at the breakfast table one morning. Nick said the same thing then, about me being "great in the kitchen." "The bread is Marc's actually," I say, hoping to take attention away from my blush. "He makes it and freezes the dough. He's brilliant at doing stuff like that."

"He's a good guy. It's so important to have good friends."

"I know it. And Marc's one of the best. So, Nick, there's this place near here called Willowmead. Marc and I go there a lot, and I used to live there for a while. It's basically a community center for gay men with HIV, and every Thursday evening there's a group of us who meet to talk. They're pretty much my family. If you think you'd be up for it, you could come along with me tomorrow. My counselor, Jarrod, leads the group, and he said he'd be happy to have lunch with you and I before, if you want."

Nick nods slowly. "I want to, yes. I mean, I want to come along with you, and I'd be happy to have lunch with your counselor, too." Nick looks down for a moment. "I think I'm having kind of a tough time with this, to be honest."

"I'm not sure there's anybody who accepts it easily, even if they try to tell themselves they do. The only thing I can say is please don't be afraid to tell me what you're thinking or feeling. It doesn't matter if it's 'the right thing to say'."

Nick takes a breath and reaches for my hand without looking. "I'm a bit scared, Pad. If we get back together, which is what I've wanted for three years now...." He swallows past the lump that's choking off his words. "I'm afraid of losing you again. All day yesterday I was just asking myself over and over, 'How could he be sick? Not now.'"

"Yeah, I know." I squeeze Nick's hand gently. "There's something kind of philosophical I've learned though. All roads lead to loss. It's true for most everything. I think it's a matter of deciding which things in life are worth the pain, you know? I mean, things that aren't worth the pain of loss are things we don't generally get attached to. Attachment, I think, is a way of acknowledging that whatever you're attached to is worth the pain of losing it one day."

Nick's eyes have gone all watery as he nods. "Yeah," he whispers. "That's true. How did you ever survive, Pad? And come through it so strong. It just... it breaks me every time I think of someone hurting you. And I can't... I still feel guilty. I should have tried harder, if I'd have pushed the police more about it, maybe they'd have found you before it got bad."

I shake my head. "I don't think they would have found me, Nick. Those two knew what they were doing. They made certain that it looked very much like I'd been living life as normal according to any records anyone had of me. It would have looked like nothing more than me staying away from what I thought was a cheating boyfriend. I was even still in touch with my mates, even if it sounded like I hated them as well."

"I know you're right. I can't help feeling like... I don't know. Maybe I just let myself fall into despair too easily. I feel like I failed you when you needed me most. Didn't you ever think it would stop, that I'd come to rescue you when I found you were gone? Didn't you... hate me when I didn't come?"

Maybe this is why we had to wait so long to find one another. Nick needs support almost as much as I did when I learned about everything. I'm in a place now where I can help with that.

"The more I think about this, the more I'm sure it wasn't just about me." I pull his hand a little closer to me. "I think they meant to hurt you as well. Maybe we'll never know why, but I think that's what they were aiming for. My mate said something to me yesterday that's true—they didn't win, Nick, we did. Maybe we're a bit banged up, but we're still here and we can keep getting stronger. They never really gained anything in the end.

"Yeah, I did think at first that you'd find me, that someone would, but they crushed that quickly. I *never* hated you though. I loved you every moment that I had any consciousness. Even when it hurt to think about you, I still did because sometimes it was the only thing I could feel, the only thing that made me think I might still be human, still a little bit me. Nick, I told you about the man who got me away from them, but it was you who kept me going long enough for him to help me. Otherwise, I don't know, I might have tried something bad."

At that incredibly poignant moment between us, the front door opens, and a pair of wankers come staggering with laughter into the entryway of my flat.

"So then the next day at rehearsal, Othello fell through the trap door that nobody bothered locking because we were all too pissed!" Freddie cackles out by the door.

Well, I suppose having a chat with Freddie and Archie to explain what's gone on is about to go out the window.

"Hey, Pad, we're staying for dinner, mate," Freddie calls.

"Um… actually, Freddie—" I call back, hoping to get him to wait a second.

"Yeah, yeah, I know you weren't planning on us. I'll do the cooking—and washing up. Why do you never have any bloody hangers in your coat closet?"

Nick hasn't said anything. He looks like he's trying to brace himself.

"Well, thanks, Fred, but I'm not sure now—"

"But nothing, mate. Don't tell me I'm gonna walk in on you and Marc in some lurid…." Freddie stops dead when he sees Nick at the kitchen table.

"Talk of lurid trysts. Look at what the fucking cat dragged in. If it isn't Nick Glenfielding." Fred's tone does not suggest a warm welcome.

"Frederick Bernard Barnes!" Marc says sternly from the way into the lounge. Any other time I would laugh at the way Marc crosses the kitchen, grabs Fred's arm, and apologizes to Nick as he drags Fred away toward his guestroom.

"Maybe I should go," Nick says quietly.

"Don't, please," I say, holding on to Nick's hand. "Marc will sort him."

"I didn't mean to cause all this."

"You didn't cause anything," I say firmly. "They intended for turmoil to divide us and our mates, they wanted to wreck everything we cared about. I was going to have a chat with Freddie about all this beforehand."

"We are back a hair early," Archie says, stepping into the kitchen. "Sorry about that."

"Don't apologize. You're just wanting to get back to Dave." I wink at him. His relationship with Dave was a real surprise, but they've been incredibly close for months now. I know what a sweet man Archie is, and I'm glad Dave has been able to trust him.

Archie gives a grin and doesn't deny my teasing accusation. "Hey, Nick. Long time, eh?"

"Yeah, unfortunately."

"Well, no time like the present," Archie says in his cheerful way. "Mind if I have a cup of that soup if we're going to have a chat, Pad? Smells just right for an autumn afternoon."

Archie sits down with a bowl. I swear he can eat at any time, through anything. He just does it automatically, and it doesn't do a thing to impede his focus on the conversation. Or his waistline, the bugger.

By the time Nick and I have gone over things, Archie just shakes his head. "Who'd have thought this was all so laid out? I guess it would have had to been. You've both come through so much, and it must have taken a lot of courage for you Nick, coming back here not knowing what you'd find."

"I don't think of it as courage," Nick says. "It was just something I had to do. If it hurt in the end, I guess I felt at the time I'd deserved it somehow."

"This isn't a just world," Archie says. "I know that too well. Neither of you deserved any of the things you've been through."

Nick nods. "I think I know that, intellectually. It's just going to take some practice with feeling it."

"Support helps. Mainly just keep things going forward and positive."

A throat is cleared over by the lounge doorway. Freddie stands there for a moment, looking a bit awkward. Marcus is standing over his shoulder, three inches shorter, and looks like he's probably poking Freddie in the back. Again, any other time, I'd be laughing my arse off.

"I, um... guess it's easy to believe something negative about someone without hearing all the facts first. And, for some of us, even easier to assume we know what's best for those we care about. So, um... I'm sorry. To both of you. Truth is, I think a part of me feels as guilty as you do, Nick. And I guess I don't deal too well with that feeling. But you weren't to blame, and it fucking sucks that you were both hurt, and.... Yeah, well, I really am sorry."

"Told you Marc would sort him." I can't help grinning. "C'mere, you wanker." Standing up I give Fred a tight hug. "I love you for your protectiveness, Freddie. I know you'll always fight for me when I need you."

"Well, I really was being a wanker just then. But after what I heard you lot tell Arch, I guess I need to be a little less reactive and work on being more responsive. I don't think any of us need any more fucking drama."

"Good job avoiding it! Didn't you say something about doing dinner, and the washing up?"

"Does that mean I'm forgiven?"

"As far as I'm concerned," I say.

"I think we were all victims of the same situation," Nick says, offering his hand to Freddie.

Freddie nods and takes it, pulling Nick up into a one-armed hug. It can only be easier from here.

Once we've all shared supper, a lot of the awkwardness has been soothed between Freddie and Nick. I don't know what Marc said to him, or if it was just hearing what Nick and I told Archie about, but I think Freddie really did regret the animosity he's held toward Nick for the last three years. When Nick and I were together they'd always gotten on well, so it's a relief to see them talking again. I know Fred's had a change of heart when he gives Nick a big hug as he's leaving with Marc and Archie.

CHAPTER 29

THURSDAY afternoon, Nick comes round to pick me up. His Land Rover is a nice ride over to Jarrod's place where we're having lunch. Jarrod, as always, leaves a unique first impression on people. He has a twisted sense of humor that can take some getting used to. Of course, Nick's sense of humor was always very dry as well, so when Jarrod asks him first off if he'd prefer a highball or a martini, Nick laughs and replies, "One each."

Of course, I was the one snickering when we all sat down together, and Jarrod started the conversation saying, "So, you're the chap who goes running down innocent letterboxes, eh?"

Nick groans. "He told you that one, huh?"

"I heard about it, though that was a long while ago now. Honestly, I don't know a whole lot about this Nick guy he's mentioned, though. And anyway, you're not all here talking to a psych doc, I'm just Pad's friend at the moment. Yeah, yeah, dual-relationship malarkey. You don't help people for years of their life without having some kind of friendship."

Jarrod is Jarrod.

It's amazing how even in his role of friend, Jarrod is able to get Nick talking about how things went and, moreover, how he was feeling.

"I don't think I've ever been so scared, frantic, as I was when it became obvious that Pad wasn't 'hiding out' with Freddie or Archie. I didn't know where he'd go. I was just so.... I tried to go to the police and tell them that something had to be really wrong, but they just told me there was nothing that could be done because Pad had been in communication with his mates and allegedly 'had a good reason to leave.' For months I tried again and again to see if any missing persons cases had turned up. Anything. Of course, after I lost my job with Serious Crimes, I didn't have the same resources on hand.

"That's when I knew I had to go back to the States, get some distance, I guess. I needed to quit drinking, too. I realized I couldn't be like that if I was ever going to find him," Nick says.

He never stopped thinking about me. Even when he had to face the fact that I either didn't want to be found, or couldn't be. I guess it was me that kept him going through his darkest moments as well.

I can see that Jarrod getting Nick to open up a bit is not just something he did for Nick, but for me also. By the time we're ready to go and let Jarrod get ready to host the meeting, I think I'm ready to let myself feel that hope I've been working to keep at bay. I know we've both been through some very serious challenges, and, in some ways, Nick and I are quite different from the people we were a few years ago. But one thing that isn't different is that we still love each other. And that love isn't based on any of the things in either of us that have changed; it's based on something that, I think, is profoundly permanent in a person.

There's still some time to go before the meeting, and as we're leaving Jarrod's, I suggest having afternoon tea at the place on South Leigh that Geoff and I like to go to. I tell Nick that I want to consider it our second "first date." The look of joy on his face as he reaches to hold my hand is worth all the first leaves of spring.

WHEN we arrive at the meeting, Freddie and Marc are there already, along with Archie who's with Dave. Mick comes up and gives me a big hug like he always does now.

"There's someone I want you to meet," I tell him. "This is Nick. Nick, Mick Carlson."

Mick gives me this long look, then gives Nick a different look before offering his hand. Despite Mick's friendly smile, I can tell his handshake comes with a bit of a warning. There's a silent exchange that goes between them when Nick meets his eyes and doesn't shy away from the handshake. Mick nods and claps him on the shoulder. Archie brings Dave over to introduce Nick, and soon they're all talking with Marc and Freddie.

Krist and Trevor are next to arrive. Krist, of course, is always quick to spot a new face in the crowd.

"Is that him?" he asks me quietly.

"I'll only answer that if you promise you won't scare him."

Krist smirks. "I promise to not scare him. No more than I scare anyone else, that is." He goes over to Nick, wraps an arm around his shoulder, and pulls him aside.

"Who's the new guy?" Trevor asks. "He seems popular."

"It's Nick."

"Oh," Trevor says. Then his eyes go wide as he realizes I mean *my* Nick. "Wow. Um… when did that happen?"

"Couple days ago. I was going to come round to talk to you, but you were apparently out late the night before."

"Wow, Pad. What's the score?"

"We'll explain," I promise him as Krist is bringing Nick back to me, in one piece, fortunately.

I'm not at all disappointed by the guys. I knew I wouldn't be. After hearing what happened to Nick as well, they have accepted him as one of our own. I think Nick had been rather braced for something on the order of the wedding dinner in *Freaks* after his chat with Krist. I've assured him that they broke the mold after they made Krist. Or more likely Krist broke it himself in coming out of the mold.

After Nick and I have talked with a few of the guys after the meeting, Nick drives me home. Pulling up in front of my flat, we just sit in the car for a couple moments before Nick reaches for my hand.

"I want to thank you," he says. "The things you've shared with me in the last couple days can't have been easy. I know you didn't know how I'd react or feel. And I imagine you're probably still getting through everything I've told you, too. Do you really want to try this, Pad? Starting over?"

"Yeah, I do, Nick. But, for a second, forget about me and tell me what you want. Now you've had a chance to see more of what you're getting into, I mean. Do you want to?"

Nick pauses for a moment and holds my hand tighter. "The way I feel hasn't changed, Padrig. I love you, positive or negative. All I want in life is the chance to be the one who's there with you, come what may. You know, I was reading something last night, written by a guy whose partner was... was dying. And there was this one line. He said no matter how much it hurt, every day, there was no way he'd miss even a moment, because at least they could hurt together."

He finishes in a rough voice, and I squeeze his hand back.

"I'm not dying, Nick. I'm quite healthy."

"I know, I want you to be, of course. I'm just saying that, no matter what happens in the future, I still believe in us and I won't back down from that. Not ever."

I lean across the center console to hug Nick. Even in that awkward position, it still feels right. I feel him exhale like it's the end of a long day and he's finally lying his head down for a rest.

"I love you, too, Nick," I whisper beside his ear. He holds on to me like he doesn't ever want to let go. Eventually we move apart, somewhat reluctantly.

"Maybe we can have dinner some night soon?" Nick suggests.

"For definite. Just tell me when and where."

"I'll ring you tomorrow, then."

"Okay." Nick stops me reaching for the handle with his hand on my arm.

"Would it be okay if I ask for a kiss? Just a small one, 'to build a dream on'?"

"Yeah, I could do that," I say with a smile.

That night, for the first time in a long, long time, I fall asleep without feeling lonely.

IT'S like learning to walk again over the next few days. The shock is beginning to wear off, my mates know what's going on, but it's a bit strange being around the man I never stopped thinking about, talking to him again, going out with him.

Our "dates" aren't exactly always normal. We went to dinner Friday evening and brunch on Sunday. Nick also comes with me to a short check-up I've got with Dr. Asha on Monday morning. He wants to be as educated as he can be; that's something that hasn't changed. This is one of those blood work appointments, and I appreciate Nick holding my hand and giving me a kiss on the cheek to distract me from the needle. It doesn't escape me that Dr. Asha is impressed with Nick. She even said to me as we were leaving that she's really happy for me and if there's anything she can do for us, just ring.

Later that afternoon I've got a tea appointment with Geoff. Nick says he'd come along for that as well, but he's meeting with the owner of that bookshop to discuss the possibility of buying it. I think it would be brilliant and tell Nick we can have dinner at the flat afterward if he wants.

Tea with Geoff goes well; everything is copacetic. He's thrilled to hear about Nick being back in the picture and is eager to meet him. Before I go, Geoff takes a small envelope from his top pocket and says he was asked to give it to me. I nearly ask by whom, but Geoff just smiles enigmatically, puts on his hat, and says, "You'll want to try the salmon pie. Cheerio!"

I put the envelope in my coat pocket and start for home. I'll open it when I get there. Nick will be over soon.

What I find when I open it is a business card for a place called Petya's Bistro on extraordinarily thick white stock with red and blue letterpress. On the back is a message in smooth handwriting:

Special dinner hours Wednesdays by arrangement. Phone and speak with Mr. Zinovyev. Welcome to bring a guest.

According to the hours on the front of the card, they aren't normally open Wednesdays. When Nick comes round I ask if he'd like to have dinner at this place on Wednesday. He's fine with that and says he can pick me up around six. Tuesday afternoon I call the number on the card to make a reservation for two, Wednesday at 6:30, name of Kennedy. I'm not surprised that the voice of Mr. Zinovyev is vaguely familiar.

I have to admit I'm a bit nervous on the ride over the next evening. I'm not exactly sure what to expect. It is strange to accept an invitation from someone I've only seen twice, doubly so when that individual is quite possibly involved in something... questionable. I meant it when I said he's something of a guardian angel though. I know for a fact I wouldn't be alive now without his intervention.

We're greeted at the door of the bistro—which is really more like a mini-banquet hall—by Mr. Zinovyev himself. He introduces himself as Kazimir and shows us to a comfortable booth.

"I am wearing many hats tonight, gentlemen. I am host, waiter, and chef for this evening. My employees are enjoying their night off. Take moment to peruse our menu, if you please."

"Geoff recommended the salmon pie," I say.

Nick nods. "That sounds good."

"Ah, yes. *Kulebyaka c lososyem* is one of our signature dishes, served with orzo. That will be good?"

"Perfect."

"Excellent. First I bring you some bread and salad. And to drink, gentlemen?"

"No alcohol, for either of us."

"Wise choice," Kazimir smiles. "I will bring best tea in house."

It's almost incongruous to see this powerful man serving guests, and I know I've only seen him a couple of times, but I have never before seen him so at ease. This is clearly what he truly enjoys most.

"Nice little place. How did you get us a special invite?" Nick asks after Kazimir steps away.

"He's an old friend," I say, leaving it at that. I'm not sure just how much I should say about Kazimir. "You know, the other day I was thinking of that night we met."

"God yes. I definitely never thought something so good could come at the end of such a miserable week as that was for me. I think I've learned that sometimes there are good things at the end of a hard road. We just have to be brave enough to get that far."

Kazimir returning just then makes me hesitate to reach for Nick's hand right away. He wasn't kidding when said he was bringing us the best tea in the house. The brown bread is also excellent. Rustic, hearty fare that is so flavorful it's almost sweet. It isn't long before Kazimir brings out the main course, and I will certainly be thanking Geoff for his recommendation. The salmon pie is out of this world. From the artistic presentation of the dish, served in the shape of a fish, to the symphonic flavor of the salmon, rubbed in saffron and basil, baked with brown rice and spinach in the puff pastry.

We're mulling over the prospect of dessert, though we're both rather full after dinner, when Kazimir returns to check on us.

"I trust everything has been satisfactory, gentlemen?"

"More than satisfactory," I say. "It was excellent."

"Good. Some people don't like that I leave out mushrooms from *kulebyaka*, but Petya never liked them. I don't keep them in stock. Am glad you were able to come tonight," Kazimir says, refilling our tea cups and pouring himself a cup as well. "I hope I might join you gentlemen for a moment."

Nick and I both nod. Nick doesn't think anything of it, but I'm dead curious about what Kazimir is going to say. He brings a chair over from a nearby table.

"Has been some time now, Padrig. Good to see you doing so well. You have beaten many odds and should be proud. And you, Mr. Glenfielding."

Nick looks a little startled, and I realize that there were no last names when we introduced ourselves. Maybe Geoff told him about Nick, though.

"I wanted to talk to you two, thought you might like to know more. Why some things happened to you both. I don't know everything myself, but I know more than I wish I did most days. Still, one must know quite a lot to remain… in good health, yes?"

Nick and I exchange looks. I was fairly sure that Kazimir knew more than a little about what went on and why. Nick has no idea, though.

"Mr. Glenfielding. You remember work you did on a case, maybe four years ago? It was against a man called Grigori, very powerful in criminal circles in this area."

"The one right before Padrig and I met," Nick says cautiously. "We put the guy away for good. Netted a lot of his buddies too."

Kazimir nods. "You did, and many people are grateful to you for that. Things are much better now than they were then. Unfortunately, some were not grateful." Kazimir looks over at me. "North and Myer. North would have been medical doctor. He never finished studies, but knew much about medicine, enough to sell drugs. Sold them with Myer for long time, ran this area's drug ring. That was until Grigori took interest. North began selling to Grigori and his 'family'. Soon he was no longer interested in dealing with individuals on streets, sold only to Grigori. When Grigori and his family were sent down, it was big loss for North and Myer. They had no other clients, not ones who bought so much. They wanted someone to pay dearly."

Nick looks as shaken as I feel. He knew the case against that man inside and out; I remember him telling me about it when we first started dating. He wrote the entire thing.

"I've never heard of 'North and Myer'," Nick says quietly. "How could have known anything about me? I was just a paralegal."

"They went after the barrister, Soames. Man you worked for. He made deal with them. Said he would give them something more valuable than his own life. He would give them man who did the work in the case… along with a 'bargaining chip' that would help them remake lost income."

Swallowing hard, I remember the Christmas do Nick and I attended for his office. I recall meeting Mr. Soames and being rather unnerved by the way he fixed his eyes on me. I thought at the time that was probably a part of what him such a good Serious Crimes lawyer.

"Please understand, I do not say these things to upset you," Kazimir assures us. "Knowledge is healing, though. There comes a time when one has seen such suffering one begins to understand, in this world, even the innocent may be forced to bear the sins of another. Neither of you are guilty, but now it is a time for you to care for one another. Be glad you have second chance. Many never even have first chance."

Kazimir is good at hiding anything he's feeling, but this time I catch a glint of sorrow and regret in his eyes. I wish I could ask him who Petya was and what happened, but I doubt he'd tell me. I can guess anyway.

"You're the man who saved Padrig, aren't you?" Nick asks.

"I helped him out of a jam once," Kazimir says, winking at me.

"Then I owe you something I can never repay," Nick says seriously.

Kazimir shakes his head. "There is no debt, not from innocent victims. I am in position to help make right of wrongs, and maybe to make right some of my own wrongs at same time. Now, you gentlemen should go and enjoy the evening. The moon is full." He winks again as he stands up and puts the chair back. "Phone any time you would like to have private dinner, will make you more *kulebyaka*."

Kazimir helps us with our coats on the way out. As he's helping me into mine I notice the barest hint of a wistful smile, and it's not just that scar.

I just have to ask, quietly. "Who was he?"

"My lover," Kazimir says. "They killed him. In front of me. To prove point. Then they gave me this." He gestures to his right cheek. "Another reason I am grateful for Mr. Glenfielding's work."

I don't say anything for a long moment. I want to hug Kazimir, but I'm pretty sure that's not his "thing." Instead I just say, "I'm so sorry for your loss," even though that doesn't come close to conveying my sympathy, or the gratitude I'm beginning to feel for knowing what it was really all about.

Kazimir nods. Then, with a small smile he says, "I am happy for your gain."

CHAPTER 31

SINCE our chat with Kazimir, Nick and I have steadily grown closer again, taking to heart his words about healing one another and making the most of our second chance. We were both able to get back on our feet while apart, but I think we both knew there was always something lacking until we found one another again.

With the help of Jarrod and the group, Nick's been able to let go of a lot of his feelings of guilt over what happened. Together we've been having fortnightly sessions with Jarrod, and it's really helped with sorting out not only what happened to us three years ago, but also where we are now and where we'd like to be down the road.

The Thursday group has become an important part of our renewed relationship as well. For Nick, it's been encouraging to see how many of the guys are in relationships, both sero-concordant and—discordant. Between seeing Jarrod and attending the meetings, I've seen Nick open up about things that I never even knew about him, like that growing up in New York, he was really insecure about fitting in and being accepted.

Things have been going well for us. Nick bought and renovated the bookshop on the corner. He reopened it as Beyond Wilde's Dreams. It's gorgeous and so inviting; he had everything redone in polished dark wood and antique-looking brass fixtures. In the front of the shop is a little tea café where people can sit with a cup and read. There's a comforting smell about the place of books, tea and milk, and lavender. I spend a lot of afternoons there, and business has been great for Nick.

I've been well. My counts are in the right places and have been holding steady. I've been pretty nearly asymptomatic and free from side effects of the meds. It is nerve-wracking every time I catch a cold, though. There's a certain sense of creeping dread, wondering if my CD4s are falling or if my viral load has spiked. It's tough when things are so unpredictable. At times I struggle with not knowing just how I was infected, by needle or sexually. I know it doesn't really make a difference, but it's just one of those things. I'll also never know exactly when I seroconverted, but Dr. Asha tends to believe it must have been rather early on, considering what the tests looked like when I was brought in to hospital. She's said that the drugs probably sped things along as well.

Nick and I have taken things pretty easy between us and continue to keep it at just dating again. We're also doing a lot of things we never got around to the first time: visiting museums, seeing more movies together, we've been to the symphony a few times and to see whatever plays Freddie is doing. Lots of "touristy" things as well. I always wanted to explore Kew Gardens, and Nick was really interested in exploring the Tower of London. He said it was for the new book he's working on, but he was rather boyishly impressed with all the gruesome torture devices. I told him he'd best not be thinking of developing a fetish.

We spent the holidays together, and that spring we starting taking some short trips together, into the countryside and down to the coast, spending weekends in quiet little cottages. For my birthday, Nick surprised me with an overnight trip to Littlecote in Wiltshire, just like he did for my birthday that year we were together.

Nick moved in with me late that summer. He was spending more nights in the guestroom than at his flat anyway. We started out sleeping in separate rooms because we'd agreed not to rush things. There was one night in the autumn when I was under the weather, though. Nick had snuggled up with me to make me feel better, and we both fell asleep like that. I woke in the night to feel him holding me and decided I never wanted that feeling of absolute security to end.

We hadn't gotten physical. We were still just sleeping, together. Not that that lasted long.

The first time… absolute disaster. It was my idea; I thought I was really ready to go there again. Nick was a little tentative and thought maybe we should talk about it more first or even consider a sex therapist. I promised him I'd be fine—frankly, I was sick as fuck of wanking when I'm sharing a bed with the man I love.

And I was fine. Nick's slow kisses—he does this thing with his tongue where he laps at mine like a kitten drinking milk—and the way he caresses my body like I'm made of silk velvet; the look of wonder and happiness in his eyes. I always felt like such a prince when we made love, and I did then too. I wanted him to make love to me like he used to.

This gripping feeling came over me when I turned on my side and he started prepping me. I had to stop him and do it myself. I was all right again once it was my own fingers doing the work. Nick was so patient, kissing and stroking my back and shoulders, whispering how much he loves me and how beautiful I am to him.

I was sure I was ready. Then I started to tremble when Nick moved in behind me and I felt his hand spreading me. Okay, I told myself, I just need to be able to see him and hold him while we make love.

Wrong again. I stopped trembling and could breathe easier once we changed positions, but it didn't last. Nick was hugging me close, our bodies in full contact. I swear I felt safe in his arms. But as soon as he started pushing in, I started to cry. It didn't hurt, I just got flooded with dark and distant, drug-hazed memories of strangers in that bedroom.

Nick stopped immediately when I took a gasping sob and hurried to get rid of the condom properly before holding me gently and whispering soothingly until I calmed down. Of course, then I started crying all over again because I was so frustrated and ashamed. For a moment I even had myself scared that he was going to tell me things wouldn't work between us after all. He said nothing of the kind, of course. In fact, what he did say was that we never had to *make* love to *have* love, that his love for me is not contingent upon sex and never was.

With help, though, we've managed to overcome even that roadblock. I wasn't ready at the time, but I did truly want to be with

Nick again sexually. In a way, it was kind of a good thing because it made me realize that I hadn't completely addressed those issues before. I've come a long way on that too, though, and now Nick and I have a happy, healthy, and satisfying sex life.

Speaking of sex lives, I think I was right about Krist developing feelings for Trevor. They seem to do almost everything together these days, though they haven't exactly come out as an item. Marc and Freddie, of course, are in it for the duration, and Archie and Dave are now living together as well. Allen is still looking, but he doesn't seem unhappy with his dating prospects; he's just enjoying the company until the "right one" comes along.

Martin is putting a lot of his time into fighting serophobia. He did end up deciding to bring a case against the firm that sacked Gier. He won, thanks to some legal advice from Nick, and the company has amended their policy. He used a part of the money he won to expand the memorial garden in the park and to plant linden trees, Gier's favorite, around it.

Mick is still on his own. I don't honestly think he'll ever be in a relationship again. Losing Oisin was an irreparable break to his heart.

It's been five years now since Nick and I found one another that rainy afternoon on South Leigh Street. Almost eight years since we were torn apart. We've made incredible progress in our lives, individually and together. We've had slips here and there, but we've always been able to pick each other back up and meet challenges head on.

There were some challenges we didn't have to meet for ourselves. Last year the restriction on HIV-positive travelers was lifted by the US, and for the first time, I visited the other side of the pond. Nick was excited to show me New York City, and we spent a week at The Plaza right on Central Park, which is breathtaking in autumn colors. We figured we were splashing out a bit with that, but then, how many honeymoons are we likely to take?

Yeah, we also got married while we were there. Because Nick also has US citizenship we were able to be married in Boston. I can honestly say that during that week, it was like there was no such thing as HIV. I was on top of the world every time I referred to myself as Mr.

Kennedy-Glenfielding. We had a big party with all our mates when we got home. The biggest wedding gift we got was when we checked out of The Plaza. Instead of being handed the bill, which we were expecting to be about 5000 US dollars, the concierge handed us a small envelope in which was a card that said:

Congratulations.

—KZ

It's a "civil partnership" here at home, but Nick and I agreed that we wanted to have the closest thing to marriage, even if it's just a matter of semantics. It's significant to us, maybe even a bit of a statement that we refuse to accept anything less than equality, but that's not really what it's about. I want people to know that Nick is my husband, that we're building a life, whether our time together is five years or fifty. I want people to know that I love him with every fiber of my being. Maybe I'm a little jealous after all, but I like it when we're at the pub and blokes eye him up, until they see that rose-gold ring on his left hand. And I want the world to know that I'm *his* for as long as I'm here.

However long that may be.

CHAPTER 32

"HEY, Pad," Nick calls to me as I'm coming in from the market. "Dr. Asha called while you were out. Your results are in."

"Thanks, babe," I call back to him, setting the bags down on the kitchen table. I can tell by the distant sound in his voice that he's tucked away in his study writing. Going in to retrieve my mobile, I kiss Nick on the cheek. "Did you kill him yet?"

"Nah. Temporary reprieve."

"That's nice, dear." Nick is so squeamish about having to kill off characters. He'll probably scrap the "reprieve" by the final draft; he's just putting it off until he can get some distance. All I know is that I love it when he writes because he's sexy as fuck in those little reading glasses.

I know he's going to be busy at the shop for the next couple days, so I figure I'll just go myself when I schedule my appointment for tomorrow.

The next day is one of those elusive sunny spring days. The breeze is warm and pleasant, and carries the scent of the flowers and trees getting green again. I pass Gier's garden on the way over to Willowmead. The linden trees have grown quite a lot, and the whole garden is flourishing, especially the lavender bushes Martin put in last year. I'm planning to stop and see Jarrod for lunch after my appointment, and I told Nick I'd probably come down to the shop for a while until he's ready to close up for the day.

By the time I've left my appointment, though, I don't feel much like eating and I'm not sure if I wish Nick had come with me or if I'm glad he didn't. I can't remember being as afraid as I am at that moment, in everything I've been through.

I go over to Jarrod's office down the hall from the medical wing, but it takes me a while to get talking to him properly. He's patient, of course, but I'm sure it's clear to him that something's not on. I spend about half an hour shrugging, nodding, and shaking my head through a one-sided conversation before I feel like I can talk about it.

"Dr. Asha had my latest blood work back," I say quietly, curled up on his couch (of course he has a "couch" in his office). "They weren't as good as they have been."

"That can happen," Jarrod nods.

"I feel fine, but… I'm scared. I mean, if this is it…. I'm not ready." I can barely talk louder than a whisper.

Jarrod reaches over to take my hand. "I'm guessing she's going to be keeping a close eye on the numbers for a couple months?"

"Yeah. She said it might have been a glitch or something. Might not be a sign of progression. I don't know if I want to tell Nick."

"Well, I can't make that call for you. But I think at this point your relationship is pretty much built on mutual trust."

"I know. I don't want him to be worried." It sounds like a weak excuse for me not wanting to face it myself.

"Maybe you could calm one another's fears?" Jarrod suggests. "Just remember, respond rather than react."

I know he's right. I need to talk to Nick when he gets home.

I don't go to the shop after leaving Willowmead, but go straight home. I'm feeling a little more in control of the situation after talking with Jarrod. Things are okay for now. Sometimes we all need a reminder that we are said to be *living* with HIV, not dying with it. I still have options open, and since I'm feeling well, making the best of everything is still a priority. I'm strong enough to face things, and with Nick's support, I know I'll get through okay.

I'm in the kitchen working on dinner when Nick gets home. He wraps his arms around me from behind as I'm putting veggies in the steamer. I turn in the circle of his arms to hold him as well.

"Thought you were planning to stop in for a while?" he asks, moving to set the kitchen table.

"Yeah, I was, but I ended up talking with Jarrod longer than I expected." I take the spoons out of Nick's hand and set them aside. "There's something we need to talk about."

Nick's brow is furrowed as I take his hand and lead him to sit with me on the couch.

"It wasn't good news from the test results. We don't know for sure, but things might be changing. My viral load was up and the CD4 count was lower this time. She wants to keep an eye on it for the next few months and see if the change continues or if it was a fluke or something."

Nick looks at me for a long moment, and I can see in his eyes that he's scared like I was earlier. Then he takes me in his arms and holds on to me. "We'll get through this, together, you and I," he says softly.

"We will. If things are changing, I can try a different cocktail. It's just a matter of watching and waiting right now."

Nick holds me close and rubs my back. We don't move apart until the kitchen timer rings twenty minutes later.

The next weeks, however, show that the tests weren't wrong. After two months of feeling like the main course at a vampire's banquet, I've finally had enough blood work done to make a conclusive call of treatment failure. Those are two of the most frightening and saddening words I've ever heard. Nick is almost more upset than I am. By this point, I'm prepared to move to other treatment options. We've been talking over the alternatives for the last couple weeks with Dr. Asha, and it seems the best course will be to change the combination pill I'm taking while keeping the other medication that appears to be still working. Once I'm started on my new meds, I'll still have to be tested frequently to make sure it's effective, but hopefully I'll be able to be back to my quarterly schedule soon. You'd think I'd get used to having blood taken after all this time, but I still feel a lot better when Nick's holding my hand.

Things don't get off to a great start though. I'd forgotten just how unpleasant the side effects can be at first. It's been years since I've had any real issue with that sort of thing, and this switch hits me like a punch in the gut. Literally. I've tried taking the meds with food and without, with certain foods and laying off certain foods, with supplements, with over-the-counter remedies, you name it. The only things I'm not doing are changing my schedule or not taking it.

I know I need to get through these side effects, though, because according to the tests the meds are working. Despite the dread I feel every time I reach for the pill bottle, I have kept perfect adherence. I'm not sure I could have done it without Nick's unflagging support, though. I swear it's a *lot* worse than the first time.

And I know Nick's worried about me. He didn't have to see me go through this with my first treatment. I'm trying to assure him that I'm all right by not changing any routines. I still do yoga on Mondays, and we still go to the Thursday meetings. I've insisted that he not change his hours at the shop. I want to keep things business as usual.

It's gotten to where I can anticipate when it's going to hit me, deal with it, and then carry on with the rest of the day. A bit like morning sickness, I guess. I'm pretty proud of myself for taking on another obstacle. That is until one afternoon after yoga.

I'd been feeling a little more tired than usual that morning, but I figured once I got going for the day and got outside I'd feel better. It was a beautiful sunny summer morning, and I did feel more energetic once I got out in the sun. The yoga session was as soothing as usual, but I was still feeling kind of lethargic afterward.

I decided to go sit in the east wing Asian garden for a while until I felt like heading home. For some reason I was having trouble catching my breath, and then I felt a wave of pain in my stomach. My ears were ringing, and I felt like I was going to pass out.

"Padrig?" I heard someone say. "Hey. What's wrong, mate? Look up at me?" Mick, if that Devon accent is anything to go by. I don't feel like I can look up at him, or even tell him what's wrong. The pain is so bad all I can do is gasp out "It hurts." I didn't even realize I was doubled over until I felt Mick put his arm around me and try to get me to sit up. I just slumped over against him.

"Fuck, Pad. I'm gonna take you in to the clinic, okay, mate?" Mick says quietly, lifting me up in his big arms without much effort.

I mumble something about feeling sick, and Mick stops dead.

"How long you been on those new meds now?" he asks urgently. I think I managed to tell him it's been a couple months because Mick turns right round and carries me out to his car in the parking lot. "I'm taking you to hospital, Pad. And *not* the one that killed my Oisin."

THERE aren't many people in the world who can say that someone saved their life. I can say that two people have. I spent several days in St. Becket's as a result of lactic acidosis, which turned out to have been caused by the new medication. Mick said it was the same thing that took Oisin. Yet again, I'm lucky to be alive.

Of course, it also means that I can't use that medication anymore. Not that I'm going to miss being sick to death, almost literally, but unfortunately my choices are getting narrower. Dr. Asha and I decide to go with a treatment a little more similar to the first one I was on, and to my eternal relief, it doesn't make me terribly ill. At least I know I won't be having adherence issues.

Nick is finally getting back to where he can stand to leave me alone for a while again. It's a bloody good thing because I was starting to get a bit miffed with tripping over him in the flat all day. I love him more than life, but I've gotten quite used to managing these things for myself. I don't need coddling when I'm feeling all right. Though I do kind of like it when I'm not doing so well, I have to admit. Really, I just want things to be normal for us. That's all.

CHAPTER 33

A FEW weeks after my stay at St. Becket's I get a call from Trevor. He's asking me to come down to the hospital as soon as I can. My first thought is that he's sick or hurt, but he says it's not for him, and please come as soon as possible. I tell him we'll be there quickly, and I go to find Nick.

Trevor meets us at the entrance, looking weary. He says he needs to talk to me for a minute. With a quick look at Nick I let him know to just wait for us and step aside with Trevor. I have a feeling I already know what he's going to say.

Some weeks ago Krist said he was going for an extended visit back to Germany. He's kept in touch, even ringing me while I was in hospital to give me a hard time. It's been about a week since I last chatted with him, though, and Trevor wasn't at last week's meeting.

"Pad." Trevor puts his hand on my shoulder. "Krist is sick. He hasn't been well for a while, refused to tell anybody though. Jarrod knows, but he's respected Krist's decision to keep it quiet. I didn't like it much, but...." Trevor gives a half shrug.

It takes me a moment. "It's bad, isn't it?"

"Yeah," Trevor whispers.

I'm trying not to get choked up as Trevor and I go back to fetch Nick. Walking up to Krist's room is difficult, seeing someone I've always known to have such hedonistic joie-de-vivre lying in a hospital bed, hooked up to monitors and IVs and having those damned breathing tubes under his nose.

"Pad-babe!" Krist smiles as I step into the room. His voice isn't anywhere near as rich as it used to be. He sounds like he's hungover from the biggest bash he's ever been to.

"Kris—" My voice is so hoarse, I'm really fighting not to lose it.

"Hey. Death is of no importance," Krist says. Even like this he's still got that blasé view of everything. "Everybody fucking does it. Of course, not everybody does it as magnificently as I." He grins, giving me that charm he uses to get himself out of—and into—anything he bloody well pleases.

Then he turns to Nick. "The threat still stands, you know. And I may be more powerful from the beyond if I have my way."

"I have no doubt," Nick says seriously before reaching out to shake Krist's hand.

I have no idea what that's all about. Probably Krist threatened to castrate Nick if he ever hurt me. That's the sort of thing I'd expect from him.

"Good," Krist says. "Now, I need you two to leave Pad and I for a bit." Nick nods and strokes my shoulder before stepping aside, but Trevor hesitates. "I am not *going* anywhere," Krist promises him with an eye roll. Trevor gives him a warning look but leans in and kisses his cheek before stepping out with Nick. I know Nick will take care of him.

"Why didn't you fucking tell me?" I ask as soon as they shut the door.

"You needed to take care of yourself, Padrig."

"Who the hell are you to talk about taking care? You'd still be healthy if—"

"I have been taking treatment for almost two years, babe. It was not enough for me, though."

"You started for Trevor, didn't you? I was really hoping to revel in this, throwing your words about not getting into a relationship back at you." Forgive my saturnine manner, but I'm torn up.

"You might recall, the reason I did not want a relationship was that I did not want to hurt my partner. As I have also mentioned, I always figured I would go big style."

I don't say anything for a while. I don't really know what to say. With everything that's been going on lately, and now Krist.

"Padrig. I do not want people to mourn me, alright? I want celebrating. Do you think I lived the way I did so people would feel terrible when I finally kicked it? Like fuck I did! I lived my way and I enjoyed every fucking minute. I made sure I did not leave any of my life left on the plate. So I do not want anyone being selfish and miserable over me."

"Krist… it's just…. I feel like everything is falling apart." Yeah, I've tried not to get upset, but this is what I feel and Krist might as well know it. "My treatment fails, then I get so sick from the second-line that I nearly end up dead myself, and now I'm losing one of the best friends I've ever had."

"I am having to say good-bye as well," Krist says quietly. And then I realize he's actually afraid, despite his bravado.

"God, Krist. I'm sorry, I shouldn't be—"

"No hiding feelings from me," he says, reaching his hand toward me. "Come sit, babe."

I take his hand and sit beside him on the bed.

"You know I love you, yes? And I always have."

I don't know when was the last time I cried like this, probably that night when I tried to snog Krist. Leaning in to hold him I try to be careful of the electrode stickers on his chest.

"Fuck them, Padrig. They aren't going to change things," Krist says, pulling me close.

"I'm going to miss you so much." I can hardly talk.

"Sei still, mein Süßer."

I HARDLY slept that night, just laid there holding Nick.

Three days later Jarrod came round to tell us.

ONCE again, I hardly have any time to recover from one grief before another comes to my door. Only a couple months after losing Krist it has become apparent that the treatment I'm on isn't doing much to hold the virus in check. My viral load continues to increase, albeit slowly, and my CD4 has gone below 200.

It's at that point that I make a decision that has been weighing on me ever since my first treatment failed. I've done all I can; I'm not going to keep this up. There isn't much left in the way of effective treatment combinations, at least ones that aren't largely experimental. I don't want to go through the blood tests, the anxiety, and the nasty side effects any more. So I'm done medicating. What's most important to me now is getting on with my life, enjoying what I can while I can, and taking what comes as it comes.

MY DECISION came closer than anything else has to breaking Nick and me apart since we found one another again. It was the only time we've ever had angry words. Ever.

He was more than hurt when I told him what I'd decided; he was furious. He couldn't understand why I was giving up on life and our life together. I heard the desperation in his voice as he argued with me and saw the heartbreak in his eyes as he all but begged me to keep trying. He wanted to take me to Sweden where they are making advances in treatment.

I was angry as well, though. I was angry that he would try to change my mind about something I've put so much energy into considering. I was angry that my treatments failed and I was getting sicker. I was angry at Krist for dying. I was angry for the death of the dream that Nick and I had so many years ago of growing old together. I was angry with every terrible thing this disease has done to me and to those I love.

My anger got the better of me, and I found myself storming out of the flat and slamming the door behind me. Unfortunately, not before I said hurtful things that I still wish I'd have left unsaid. Like that Nick should get the fuck out of our relationship before things got too hard for him to take. I shouted at him that I wasn't going to live forever and he'd better start living with that reality. I didn't even make sense to myself when I said he was being selfish, wanting to keep me alive and sick, and then in the next breath I called him a vulture and accused him of just hanging around waiting for me to die.

Nick looked devastated. I'm ashamed to admit I was momentarily pleased by that, but even as I stormed away I hated myself for hurting him. I was down to South Leigh by the time I really broke down. I was almost hysterical and getting some really weird looks, but there wasn't a thing I could do to stop it. I went down to Gier's garden, curled up on a bench under one of the lindens, and wept. It was as bad as when I thought Nick had cheated on me.

After a while, I even felt someone's hand on my shoulder. Only instead of that bastard Bennett, it was Jarrod who wrapped his arm around me and pulled me close. Neither of us said anything. Once I calmed down a bit, he offered to walk home with me, and I just nodded. On the way, Jarrod kept his arm around my shoulders while I explained what happened. He didn't say he "knew" or "understood." He just listened.

As soon as I walked back into the flat, I saw Nick sitting huddled up at the end of the couch. When he looked up at me, his eyes were red and puffy. Just like mine were, I'm sure.

"Nick...." My voice was all raspy. He rushed over to hold me. "I'm so sorry... please...."

"No, Pad, *I'm* sorry." He was faring no better. "You were right, it's your decision to make and I... I was being selfish. I'm just scared, Padrig, because... I love you so much."

"Oh, Nick. I don't want you hurting like this." It was tough to talk around sniffling. "Maybe... maybe you should think about it, I wouldn't be angry if you do want out."

"No!" Nick cried. "Never!"

"I don't want you remembering me as weak and sick."

"Pad, that's not how anyone's going to remember you, least of all me," Nick said softly. "You're so strong and brave, I don't know how I'm going to have any strength without you."

"Maybe we're one another's strength, yeah?"

"Yeah," Nick echoed.

Jarrod stepped into the lounge from the kitchen with a pot of tea and three mugs, and suggested we all have a sit. He said we might consider doing regular sessions with him again, since there's such a unique set of issues that comes with full-blown AIDS.

CHAPTER
34

I'VE had some things to deal with. I'm tired a lot, having anemic blood; almost perpetually have colds; my skin breaks out in rash at the drop of a hat; I have a tough time keeping my weight up; some days it's a challenge standing too long or walking too much, and more often these days I need Nick's help getting up the flight of stairs to our flat—achy joints are a bitch. It's annoying as fuck, but I have to say that I'd feared far worse. I've come to just live with it.

I think it's harder on Nick. I don't think he hides his feelings from me; he's honest with me about the things that are harder for him, like seeing me losing weight or the coughing fits I sometimes take. But there have been times I've drifted awake in the night without him noticing, only to find him curled beside me and sobbing silently. I know his heart breaks a little more every day, and I know there's nothing I can do to make it better.

Nick's been wonderful, really, he's always just what I need at the moment—supportive, gentle, understanding, relaxed; a distraction, a jester, an audience to my complaints. Most of all he's been the arms that aren't afraid to hold me close and the lips that aren't afraid to kiss me. And yes, the hand that isn't afraid to touch me intimately. I never thought it would be important to feel sexually desirable at this point in my life, but Nick makes me feel like I'm still porn-star hot. The feeling is quite mutual.

There was one time when we were making dinner together. The knife slipped and caught the end of my finger. It was just a small scratch, but it did bleed a bit. I dropped the knife in the sink and reached to turn on the hot tap with my other hand. Nick reached to take my cut hand in his, and I shouted, "No!" I was immediately terrified of the idea of him touching even a few drops of my blood.

Nick looked at me with such calm love in his eyes. He just held my hand under the running water for a moment and put a little antibiotic cream and a plaster on it for me, barely taking his eyes from mine. Then he kissed it and held me close for a long while. I've never felt as accepted as I did in that moment.

All that aside, I'm still enjoying life. Nick and I don't travel very much now. Going into downtown London once in a rare while is about as much as I'm up to, and even that wears me out for a couple days. I'm okay with it. We got in quite a lot of travel after our New York honeymoon—Paris, Sitges, Bruges, Amsterdam. We even spent an incredible week in Vanuatu for our first anniversary. The flat is filled with so many photos from beautiful places, from iridescent viridian islands to ancient and sophisticated cities, and us in them. We made it a point to keep our travel gay-friendly; I'm *not* not holding his hand!

We do actively appreciate all the beautiful things in life, though— music, art, books, plants, breezy sunny days, gentle stormy nights, subtle sunrises, blazing sunsets, and velvet-teal, silvery full moons. Most of all, one another. We aren't wasting a moment.

I'm not unhappy. I've known unhappiness, and these days, while challenging to say the least, couldn't hold a candle to what I've been through before. Mostly because I didn't have Nick with me during that time. Through it all I've kept positive. Sorry, sero-joke.

Just because I've decided to go off HAART meds doesn't mean I'm not taking anything at all. I take meds to manage what symptoms I've had and to stave off opportunistic infections that are just gagging to get to me. The meds I'm taking now are pretty low risk for side effects and seem to be doing their job.

I think one day HIV will no longer be as virulent and destructive as it is. Smallpox is almost unheard of in the developed world today, and even flu is generally considered little more than a nuisance for most people. I have the feeling that the virus will naturally wear itself down before an effective cure is ever produced. There's a lot of money in medications that keep you alive long enough to keep taking medications, and I know very well just what depths people can go to over money. I also know and do not take for granted just how fortunate I am not only to have a source of means but also to live in a nation where my medical care is so accessible.

We still go to the Thursday meetings every week. There are fewer of us than there were when I first came to Willowmead. It was several months after Krist's passing that Clyde made the ultimate decision. His health had been deteriorating for a while. When he began experiencing some early signs of dementia, he knew he didn't want to wait to get to a point where he didn't recognize Christian anymore. I think that's probably the most feared complication of AIDS; I know it's my greatest fear. I cried a river when Christian told us about holding onto Clyde as he took the pills and then lying down with him for the last time.

There is one decision I've made about which I am adamant. I will not, under any circumstances, die in hospital. I'll go in for treatment if I need to; I'm sure I will at some point, likely more than a couple times. But I've made it plain to Dr. Asha and Nick that when there's really nothing left to do and I say I want to go home, they'd bloody well better not argue with me. I will experience death on my own terms and no one else's.

You see, Krist and I disagreed about the "importance" of death, though I know that was just his bravado talking. Death is of great importance, for those facing it sooner than later as well as for their loved ones. It's probably one of the greatest things we ever undertake. I'm not afraid of dying, or of whatever sickness will finally take me. I do not want to leave my friends or Nick, either. I don't know what comes after all this, but I'd like to hope that I'll be able to pick up right where I left off, in a better existence where people don't harm one another and there are no diseases—just love and friendship, music and laughter, and, if there is any justice, good food and drink as well. And a lot of sex.

It is my hope that despite all the trials and tribulations you've shared with me, you might have come away with a sense of hope. No matter what obstacles you must confront in life, you can overcome them. Those that cannot be overcome can be managed. Everyone has that sort of strength, and I wish everyone the clarity of mind and heart to be able to know their true strength when they have need of it.

There are no easy roads, my friends. The only thing that gets us through it all is love. So, love too many people too deeply. Don't be too quick to react or judge others, because appearances are often deceiving and we can't know what road someone else has traveled to get here. And never be afraid to let someone love you; you deserve it more than you know. But more than anything, love yourself. No matter how much others love you, no matter how they would do anything for you, there may be times when through no fault of yours, you might be the only person you can rely on when you are faced with bearing the sins of another.

To my friends, to those who have saved and preserved my life, and most of all to Nick: I love you in ways I can never rightly express. I only hope that you all know it. My gratitude is eternal.

Allen—one of the first to offer me a warm welcome to Willowmead when I was uncertain and needed mates more than anything.

Archie—who I can always count on to understand and make me smile, no matter what.

Dr. Asha—for giving me the information I needed to make my own decisions and for respecting those decisions, for all you've done to keep me well over the years, and for believing in me when I least believed in myself.

Christian and Clyde—the first example I saw of a deeply loving "magnetic" couple, who gave me hope that a seropositive man could be loved as much by a seronegative man as any.

Dave—for his courage in overcoming a terrible betrayal to find love and trust again.

Freddie—who I know will always stand up for me.

Geoff—the ultimate social advocate and liaison to my financier, as well as a good mate who knows exactly what a good cup of tea is all about (and knows that a string and a paper tag are "in case of emergency" only).

Jarrod—who always knows just what to say and when there's nothing to be said. Without you I would never have gotten to where I am today.

Kazimir—my guardian *angelsk*.

Krist—who, never doing anything by half-measures, was one of the best friends a bloke could ever have. You showed me what it meant to beat an unbeatable disease. You are unforgettable, Krist-babe, and I always loved you as well.

Marcus—who showed me that it's all right to make an unpopular decision when it's what's right for you. You gave me every example of how to take good care of myself. Your Jamey was a lucky man, as lucky as our Freddie is.

Martin—a quiet, kind man who stands firm for what's right. Gier would have been proud of the support you've shared with those who need it most and the work you've done for justice.

Mick—one of the men to whom I owe my life, even though you insist we're square for all the times you cried on my shoulder. Your Oisin must have been all the wonderful things you've said he was to have won the heart of our big teddy bear.

Trevor—Finley would have been proud of you. Krist was, and I am as well.

And to Nick—the love of my life. And if I have anything to say about it, my afterlife as well.

EPILOGUE

WE'D moved from the flat about a year and a half earlier. It was tough on Pad going up to the first floor, and he'd always wanted a garden or patio. We found a nice bungalow not too far from Willowmead, and Archie and Dave became the next to "inherit" the flat. Here, all the necessities are accessible on the ground floor; it was a lot easier for Padrig.

It's been six months. Padrig was having a difficult bout of coughing fit one evening and then said that there was pain in his chest. I wasted no time getting him to St. Becket's. He was rushed in and a few hours later we were told it was PCP—pneumocystis pneumonia. They could keep him in for a few days, hit it with some antibiotic, and see how it responded. Padrig nodded and told me to go on home and sleep.

Not a bloody chance I was leaving that hospital! I'd promised not to argue him when he said he wanted to go home, but I never said *I* was going to go home when he told me to.

"I'm okay, Nick," he promised me in a thin, tired voice. "I just want you to rest, baby."

"I'll rest here. I'm not going anywhere. I can sleep in a chair, but I wouldn't get any sleep at home without you."

Padrig sighed. "You'll have a stiff neck, probably a sore back as well."

"Yep. It'll loosen up; take a paracetamol if I need it."

"You're a stubborn old bastard." He smiled at me though, like he was hoping I'd stay after all and was just protesting for show. "Why don't you at least get yourself a cuppa?"

"Maybe. Anything you want?"

He closed his eyes for a few moments and then reached for my hand when he opened them. "Yeah. I want to go home."

The way he said it, the way he looked at me... I knew he wasn't just whinging about having to be in hospital.

"Now?" I sounded like someone had their hands around my throat, and it felt like it.

Padrig shook his head. "No. Not immediately. In the morning, though."

In the morning? Was he suggesting that I might only have another twelve hours with my partner? I had to try not to panic.

He held my hand tighter like he was reading my mind, though it was probably all over my face, clear as day. "It's okay, Nick. Not yet. I promise. Let's just get some rest. God, I hate these bloody pillows, want my six inches of down."

"Six inches I can provide, but I figured you'd want it up, not down." Pretty weak attempt, I know.

"Hospital sex has never been on my list. I'm a little tired at the moment, but you can have a wank if you really want. I could watch, I'm not bothered." His grin is still as sweet as ever.

"Yeah, that'll be brilliant when the nurses rush in because I've sent you into a spasm or something."

"Okay, we'll save it for home."

I didn't get any real sleep that night. I drifted off a few times in the little reclining chair beside Pad's bed, but every time someone walked by the room I woke up thinking it was a team coming to revive Pad. Dr. Asha came by around nine in the morning, and I was hoping she'd tell Padrig it wasn't at all to the point of "going home." She didn't, just took his hand and nodded, saying she'd have the release papers done at once. We were home by ten.

I was grateful for the extra help down at Wilde's over the next couple days. I had myself on the rota, but Dave was happy to cover the schedule. A number of the guys from Willowmead came round to visit Pad; he'd invited them himself. Marcus, Freddie, Archie, and Trevor were here the most.

By the fourth day, Padrig seemed to be picking up, and I started to feel relieved. I'd hardly slept the last few nights and was falling asleep in the middle of the day more than I ever have. I figured the antibiotic was working and we'd dodged yet another bullet. I actually got some sleep that night and was thinking of dashing down to the shop for a bit the next day, just to make sure all was going okay.

It was still dark when I woke to Padrig getting out of bed. I was going to help him to the toilet, but he said he wanted to go out on the patio and watch the sunrise. It was a fair morning but still a bit chilly. Pad was wrapped up in his flannel pajamas, fleece dressing gown (the same one he loaned me that evening we were caught in the rain), and those fuzzy socks that are his favorite. We went into the back garden with a couple mugs of tea and a rainbow afghan, and sat down together on the divan-sized porch sofa.

We're on a hill, and our garden has a view of the park over which the sun rises. Padrig's always loved having a quiet morning like this, sitting outside with a cup of tea, watching the new day dawn. Most of the time I was sound asleep until nearly noon. Of course, early on we shared more than a couple sunrises getting back in from parties. It was beautiful that morning, a blazing pink and orange sky, streaked with narrow bands of gray clouds, over the misty trees in the park, with a swath of robin's-egg blue through the middle. It made me wish I was a painter or photographer, but it's as vivid in my memory as if I had painted it.

Padrig and I stretched out, and I held him cradled against my side. We talked quietly about nothing in particular for maybe half an hour as the sun climbed and the mist gradually retreated. A raspy-voiced magpie on our roof chattered with another over in the park.

"I'm thinking of looking in on the shop later today," I mentioned.

Padrig was quiet for a minute and then said, "Stay a little longer?"

"Yeah, of course." I ran a hand over his hair. "No rush."

"I think this is the loveliest morning I've ever had," Padrig said with a contented smile and snuggled in closer to me.

He was quiet for a while longer, and I wondered if he'd fallen asleep again. That tended to happen.

Then he stirred a little. "Love you, Nick," he sighed.

"Love you too, babe."

Padrig was quiet again after that.

JESSICA SKYE DAVIES has been a writer since her first works were "published" in her grandparents' living room and written in crayon. She is a lifelong native of Pittsburgh, Pennsylvania, where she has been active in the community, including serving as library director on the executive board of a local GLBT community center. Outside of writing, Jessica has a wide range of interests and hobbies: from Mozart in a music hall to punk in pubs, from Shakespeare to Vonnegut, from salsa dancing the night away to afternoon coffee in the square to kicking back with a good movie. She loves meeting new people and exploring new places, always open to whatever elements might inspire her next writing project.

Visit Jessica at:

Blog: http://jessicaskyedavies.blogspot.com

Facebook: http://www.facebook.com/jessicaskye.davies

Also from JESSICA SKYE DAVIES

http://www.dreamspinnerpress.com

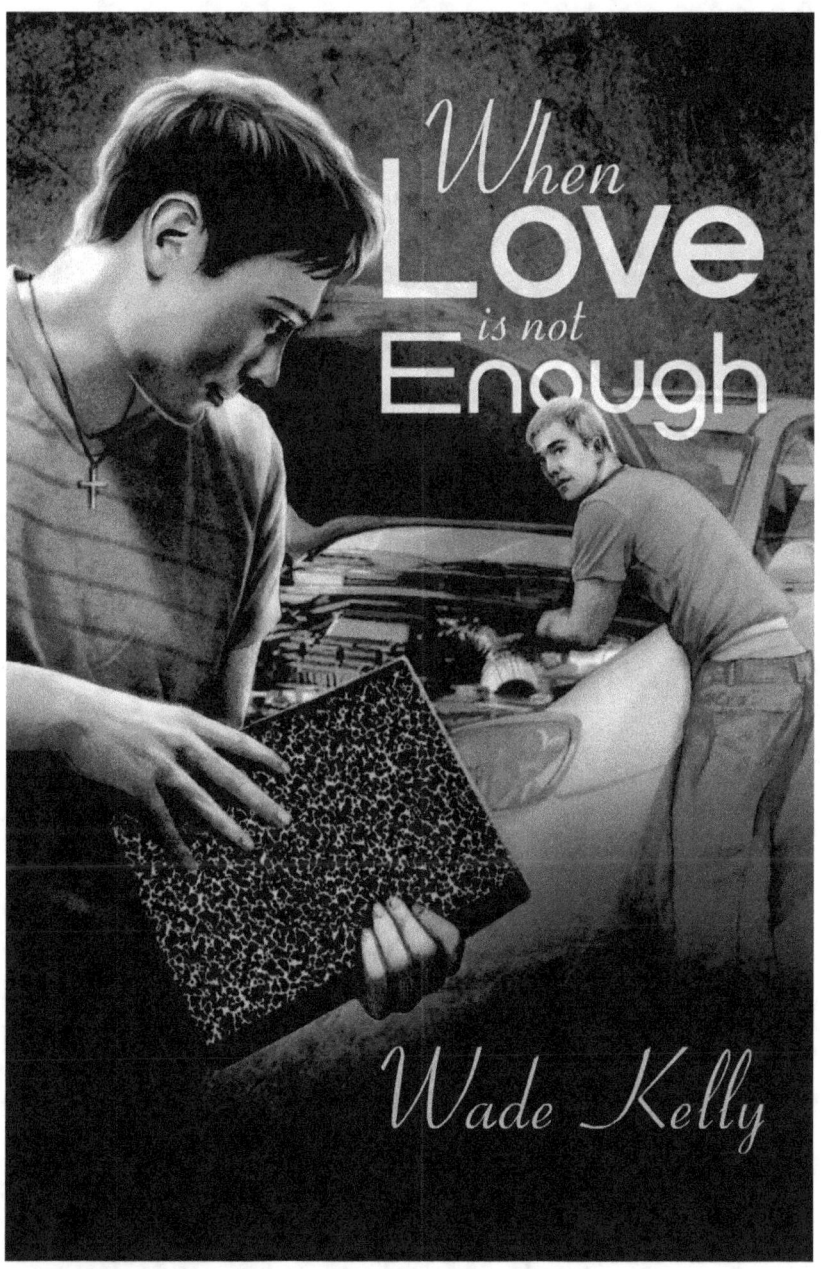

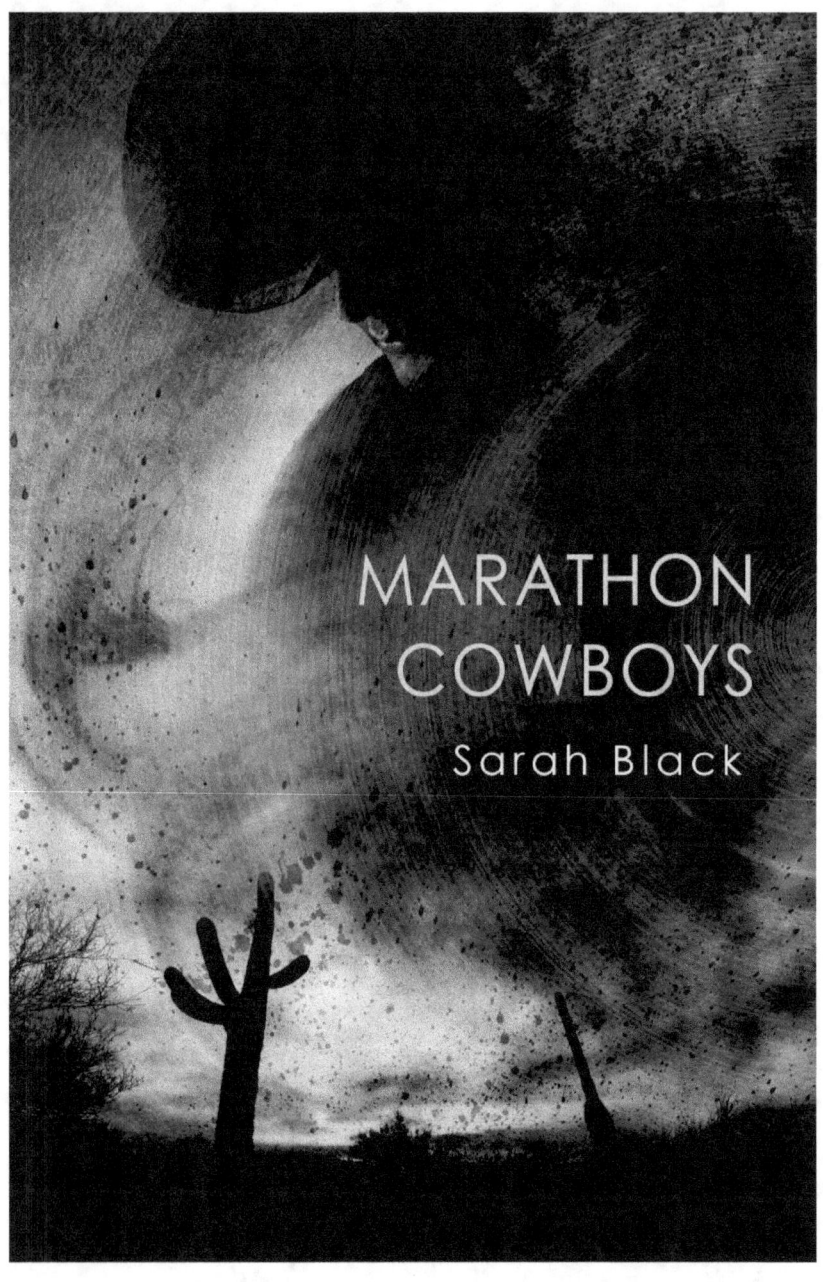

A SLICE OF *Love*

ANDREW GREY

www.ingramcontent.com/pod-product-compliance
Lightning Source LLC
Chambersburg PA
CBHW070117260626
47160CB00004B/1507